Praise for
Boo Humbug

"Move over Dickens, there's a new Scrooge in town. Of course, this one may be heading for a straitjacket. With *Boo Humbug,* Rene Gutteridge serves up a romping good read that alternately had me scratching my head and chuckling. And just when I thought the tale had reached its peak—a surprise ending that delivers the Christmas message with feeling."

—TAMARA LEIGH, author of *Splitting Harriet*

"A touch of eccentric, a measure of Dickens, and a generous dollop of love, and you have the perfect recipe for Christmas. *Boo Humbug!*"

—DIANN MILLS, author of *When the Nile Runs Red*

"What fun! I enjoyed *Boo Humbug* from the first page to the last. With characters that come alive and a storyline full of clever turns, it had me chuckling, cheering, and even reaching for a tissue at the end. I think I'll have to start a new Christmas tradition—reading Rene Gutteridge's *Boo Humbug.* I loved it!"

—MARLO SCHALESKY, author of five books, including *Veil of Fire*

"Only in Skary, Indiana, would a simple production of *The Christmas Carol* devolve into a hilarious disaster. With her trademark blend of insight and wit, Rene Gutteridge's return to Skary is funny, heartwarming, and an absolute delight to read."

—MELANIE DOBSON, author of *Together for Good* and *Going for Broke*

“In *Boo Humbug,* Rene Gutteridge and her lovable cast of characters present a story of Christmas unlike any other. Charming, witty, and fun, this tale promises to delight readers for years to come.”

—DIANN HUNT, author of fourteen novels,
including *Be Sweet*

BOO HUMBUG

Novels by Rene Gutteridge

My Life as a Doormat

The Boo Series

Boo

Boo Who

Boo Hiss

Boo Humbug

The Occupational Hazards Series

Scoop

Snitch

The Storm Series

The Splitting Storm

Storm Gathering

Storm Surge

Boo Humbug

Christmas Is Scarier
Than You Think

Rene
Gutteridge

WaterBrook
Press

Boo Humbug
Published by WaterBrook Press
12265 Oracle Boulevard, Suite 200
Colorado Springs, Colorado 80921
A division of Random House Inc.

ISBN 978-1-4000-7353-5

Published in association with the literary agency of Janet Kobobel Grant, Books & Such, 4788 Carissa Avenue, Santa Rosa, CA 95405.

Library of Congress Cataloging-in-Publication Data
Gutteridge, Rene.
Boo humbug : a novel / Rene Gutteridge. — 1st ed.
p. cm.
ISBN 978-1-4000-7353-5
1. Indiana—Fiction. 2. Christmas stories. I. Title.
PS3557.U887B6635 2007
813'.54—dc22
2007021314

Printed in the United States of America
2007—First Edition

10 9 8 7 6 5 4 3 2 1

TO ALL THOSE WHO LOVE SKARY, INDIANA,

AS MUCH AS I DO.

CHAPTER 1

> "What's Christmas time to you but a time for paying bills without money; a time for finding yourself a year older, but not an hour richer; a time for balancing your books and having every item in 'em through a round dozen of months presented dead against you? If I could work my will," said Scrooge indignantly, "every idiot who goes about with 'Merry Christmas' on his lips, should be boiled with his own pudding, and buried with a stake of holly through his heart."

"THINK OUTSIDE the box," Mr. Watson implored as his gaze fell over his students, all clustered together on the stage floor, their backs erect with enthusiasm. Lois Stepaphanolopolis was the only one not sitting on the floor. She'd tried it once, but her hips hurt for a solid seven days afterward, so now she used a chair and a comfortable slump. She watched Mr. Watson gesture toward an imaginary audience. "Give them something they're not expecting!"

His voice held an authoritative nobility, and he looked down his nose at his students. Lois was the oldest by at least thirty years. The rest were barely out of high school, had somehow missed out on college for one reason or another, and now bet their dreams on one community college class.

Lois wasn't that naive. She didn't dream of going to New York and starring on Broadway. She was too old for that kind of grand self-deception. But she did have her little theater company, and they'd had quite a nice summer producing one-acts.

Yet something was tugging at her creative conscience. She couldn't really identify it, but it kept her awake at night, dreaming of bigger and better. She knew she had it in her to do more—to rise higher—but with what? Which story needed to be told?

Mr. Watson's sparkling blue eyes studied each face with great dramatic pause, just like he'd taught them. "Don't be afraid of silence on the stage. Embrace it. Use it to its full benefit. Sometimes silence is more powerful than words. Don't let it linger too long. But if you use it just right, it can be the perfect punctuation to a piece of dialogue that was meant to change the world."

Lois smiled at the thought. Never had she imagined theater could change the world, but the more she did it, the more she understood how much people craved entertainment and the enlightenment that often came from it.

Lois's hand popped up right as Mr. Watson started to describe the finest moment in his stage career. He blinked a couple of times, as if a bright light were aimed at him. "Yes, Ms. Stepaphanolopolis? What is it?"

"I'm going to do it!"

"Do what?" Mr. Watson asked.

"Conceive! Outside the box!"

Mr. Watson glanced around at all the students, then back at Lois. "I'm assuming we're not talking about in vitro fertilization here?"

Lois laughed. Mr. Watson was terribly witty. "That's what you've been telling us all week. Don't do it like everyone else does it. Bring something new to the table, right?"

"You've been listening," Mr. Watson said, with a mild smile. "Good for you."

"Not just listening, Mr. Watson. Obeying! I can hardly sleep at night. I think I have an idea. A really great idea. An idea that no one in the history of the world has ever thought of."

"Hmm." Mr. Watson looked skeptical but amused. "Lois, I'm thankful you're implementing what I've been teaching you. I encourage every student to think outside the box. It's what makes great characters. When you're tackling a role, remember to bring your own version to the table and—"

"Bigger!" Lois spread her arms wide. "Not just the characters, but the *story.*" She closed her eyes, her face turned up toward the stage lights. "I'm going to do something that's never been done before."

A few people snickered. Lois dropped her arms and looked at them. *Jealous.* The youngsters didn't have the experience she had. They couldn't go to the places she could.

Mr. Watson cleared his throat. "That's terrific, Lois."

Lois stood and gathered her things. "I have to go now."

"Class isn't over," Mr. Watson said.

"I know, but I have a lot of work to do. You, of all people, Mr. Watson, understand that once...maybe twice...in a lifetime, brilliance strikes in such a way that everything must come to a stop until the vision has been fulfilled."

Mr. Watson raised an eyebrow.

"Oh, all right," Lois said, smiling demurely. "If you must know."

"Must know what?"

"I'm doing Dickens." She paused, letting the silence do the talking. When it'd had its effect, she cut it off and said, *"A Christmas Carol."*

Mr. Watson hushed the sudden flurry of snickering.

"What?" Lois asked with a frown.

A bobble-headed blonde, otherwise known as Staci, said, "You're kidding, right? I mean, if there's ever been a Christmas play that's overdone, it's that. It's been done thirteen billion times as a play, and at least a million times as a movie. It's been done on television, on radio, in the park, off Broadway, on Broadway—"

"Every way possible," another student interrupted.

Lois folded her arms together and narrowed her eyes. Poor Mr. Watson. No wonder he appeared so aggravated all the time. At first, it seemed like he didn't want to be teaching at a community college, but upon further observation, surely the cause was the narrow-mindedness of today's young people. She gave Mr. Watson a knowing glance. "They have a lot to learn, don't they, Mr. Watson?"

She threw her scarf around her neck. "I bid you farewell and lots of luck in your future careers as waiters and waitresses."

Staci smirked. "Please. You really think you can do theater better than the rest of us? Give me a break. No offense, lady, but you're from a small town, and you're way over the hill—and in over your head. You're the one person here who never seems to know what's going on."

Lois looked at Mr. Watson, whose understanding expression tried to compensate for Bobblehead's attitude. "Lois, I'm glad you're trying to think outside the box. It's a huge improvement. Wasn't it just last week that you walked out of the improv lesson because you thought it was a waste of time, since actors always use scripts?"

"Thank you for your confidence, Mr. Watson," Lois said. "And I can assure you, *A Christmas Carol* has never been done like this." She addressed the students. "Wait and see. It will be unforgettable." She slid her arms through her coat sleeves, buttoned the front, and walked off the stage, her heels clicking loudly until she reached the carpet of the center aisle, where she marched forward. And with each step, one thought built onto another, forming a tower of brilliance. She stopped at the front doors of the auditorium and smiled to herself. Everything came together inside her head. She knew exactly what she wanted to do and how she would do it.

Alfred Tennison strolled along the leafy path that wound through the woods just north of his rental house. It was actually the only house in Skary, Indiana, to rent. People either lived and died here or didn't come at all. And he wasn't sure why he always felt the need to return. Since crashing and burning in publishing, first as Wolfe Boone's editor and later as his agent, Alfred's career had improved slowly but steadily.

Now he worked as a freelance editor, pulling in enough to afford a modest apartment in Manhattan. Sometimes, for no reason he could identify, he came back to Skary and stayed for indefinite periods of time.

He'd started morning walks a while back when he was trying to get a grasp on the string of life that was quickly unwinding around him. Then he added one after lunch. Now he walked in the evenings too. It made him feel kind of old. Back in New York, he used to feel almost repelled by the sight of old people walking the sidewalks and the parks. He wondered if it was the most exciting part of their day and the only time that they were near other human beings before returning home to eat their dinner at four and turn in at seven.

He also would've never guessed he'd be ambling through a forest at night. In New York, it could be risky even walking in a well-lit park during the day. But the woods seemed to be the only place in town where Christmas lights couldn't be seen. The town had them strung up the flagpoles and down the light poles, around every government building, through the town hall, and over the roof of any building with access to electricity. They popped up overnight the day after Thanksgiving and would stay up until after the new year. It was no lie—on a moonless night in mid-December, if you walked down Main Street, you might think it was noon.

But it wasn't just the Christmas lights. If that were all he had to consider, maybe on some level, he might be able to tolerate it. However, Christmas cheer wasn't confined to decorations. It was the attitude of the entire town, as if life weren't fully lived until you wore a Santa sweater and joined a Christmas carol touring group. If you had no desire to gush about pumpkin pie and Aunt Betsy's turkey, it was hard to find common ground.

Even Wolfe, his longtime friend, seemed to have converted. Back in the normal days, when Wolfe was a famous horror novelist nicknamed Boo, Alfred was successful and wealthy by association. Christmas was a party, not a religious event, and there seemed to be little to worry about. Alfred recalled that even before Wolfe was struck down by religion, he wasn't that into the festivities. But it didn't much matter—Alfred carried on the festivities without him. There were corporate cocktail parties, VIP dinners, shopping for people he wanted to impress, and receiving gifts from people who were in desperate need of him in one form or another. Champagne and caviar, limos and fancy suits, mingling, laughing, toasting success and successes to come.

But now he couldn't remember the last time he'd been to a party in New York. And the only people he received gifts from were Wolfe and his wife, Ainsley. Champagne, the kind he *would* be caught dead drinking, was too expensive. And those friends who used to toast him were inaccessible until he regained his former status.

Now he was in Skary, walking along a dirt path and trying his best to maintain his subgrade life in a manner that kept him from staying in bed all day long. He returned cheery greetings the best he could and tried to conduct himself in a way that didn't raise suspicions about his dislike for a yearly holiday that seemed more like a global event.

He came to a clearing where he had a nice view of the town below. The wind snapped through the trees and chilled his skin. There sat Skary in all its glory, encircled by a halo of light. Cars crept by like there was not a single important place to be. People greeted the cold like it was a warm friend, skating on the ponds, laughing on the street corners, window-shopping with barely a dollar to their names.

Alfred put his hands deep inside the pockets of his coat and tried to remember what the town was like a few years ago, when tourists drove for miles to see the house on the hill at the opposite end of town. From where Alfred stood, he could see yellow light glowing from every window of that old house, the one that looked fit to regurgitate every terrible and horrifying tale that came from an imagination that never ended.

Until one day it did. At least in a monetary sort of way. Wolfe

Boone, horror novelist extraordinaire and the one success Alfred could take complete credit for, decided he needed more meaning in his life. At first, Alfred chalked it up to writer's block, but he soon made the dreadful discovery that Wolfe had met Jesus. Suddenly the *New York Times* Best Seller List ceased to be important to Wolfe.

But it never did cease to be important to Alfred.

Sighing, Alfred pulled the collar up around his neck and turned back toward the rental house, plodding along, kicking dead leaves to either side of the path. December was a long month, and he would be glad when it ended. Except then a new year would begin, and he couldn't help but wonder what part of his life he would lose next in another turn of bad luck.

CHAPTER 2

Darkness is cheap, and Scrooge liked it.

THE CLOCK READ 4:38 a.m., and the night was as frigid as her Frigidaire, but neither sleep nor cold could stop her. Lois had been writing nonstop, starting in the early afternoon and continuing into the evening, when she paused only to eat soup and drink milk. Then the writing resumed, and here she was, one arm wrapped along the top of the pad of paper while the other feverishly scribbled down every thought that popped into her head. Never had she experienced anything like it—her brain bubbled over with brilliance that couldn't be contained.

For a moment she stopped, rubbed her eyes, and rose to make a fresh pot of coffee. She couldn't remember the last time she'd gone without sleep. She thought it impossible, since long ago she'd convinced herself that she was not fit for less than nine hours of sleep. Usually, her entire day revolved around making sure she got a good night's sleep and if not, then at least a three-hour nap during the day.

The coffee began to drip through the filter, filling the kitchen with an aroma that motivated Lois to return to her work. Something was driving her to finish. She must finish it! There was little time to waste. By sunrise, she would have it complete, and then—she knew deep in her heart—Skary, Indiana, would never be the same.

With a heavy blanket and their comforter laid perfectly straight across his body, Wolfe stared at the ceiling, wondering why he was hallucinating. He'd only hallucinated one other time, when he'd accidentally taken too much cold medicine on an empty stomach. He'd lain on his couch, nursing his aching body with everything from soup to ginger tea, wondering how that bird had gotten into his house and why it liked to fly upside down. It wasn't until the next day that he realized there was no bird, and the bottle said two *teaspoons,* not two *tablespoons.* That error, mixed with a high fever, had managed to conjure up some very strange images.

But he hadn't taken any cold medicine tonight, and as far as he could tell, he wasn't sick. Exhausted, yes. Sick, no. He closed his eyes and listened again. There it was, soft but distinct.

He couldn't help but sigh. Loudly. Loudly enough that Ainsley moaned beside him and then put a gentle elbow in his ribs. He threw back the covers, sat up, slid his feet into his slippers, and willed himself to stand. But there he sat, hunched over and staring at a floor that went in and out of focus.

"Wolfe," Ainsley said, her voice full of grogginess, "what are you doing?"

"Just making sure."

"Just making sure of what?"

"Never mind." Wolfe managed to stand. His knees actually felt a little weak, but then again, he wasn't used to pacing so much. He plodded down the hallway toward the room on the other side of the house. It was a short walk, except at night, when it felt like miles.

Through the crack of the slightly open door, he could see the moon's light washing over the dark wood floors. And in the corner, a little movement. He wasn't hallucinating. She was awake. For the third time in one hour.

He eased the door open and walked to the crib. Abigail noticed him and stopped her crying for a moment. Wolfe reached down, and she tried to grab for his finger. When she couldn't, she shut her eyes and cried as loud as a little person could cry.

"Oh, now, come here," Wolfe said gently, picking her up and then cradling her in his arms. Satisfied, she stopped crying, but her eyes popped open so wide Wolfe had to smile. Any time she had a chance of staying awake, she gave it her all. "How can you be awake? I just put you back to sleep twenty minutes ago." Her wide eyes blinked at him through the darkness. "You're not going back to sleep, are you?" Abigail cooed, and he wondered how he was even able to smile. He'd never felt so tired in his life. A few well-meaning locals had warned him of the sleep deprivation to come, but thinking back on it, they had understated it.

He took Abigail downstairs, walking gently so as not to wake Ainsley. They'd come up with a system whereby Ainsley took the first "shift" and Wolfe took the second. It was fair in all regards, but he couldn't help feeling a little animosity toward her, simply because she was sound asleep, warm under the covers, and he was nodding off while walking down a flight of stairs.

He made it to the kitchen where Abigail watched with seeming thoughtfulness as he, using one hand, managed to scoop the coffee into the filter and turn the coffee maker on. There was no use sitting down. As soon as he did, she would start wailing. He glanced at the clock. She wouldn't be fed for another hour, so all he had to do was wait and hope he didn't faint from fatigue.

While the coffee took its time dripping into the pot, Wolfe walked and bounced, walked and bounced. What a delight this little girl was in his life, even when he felt like he might die if he didn't get a chance to shut his eyes for a few minutes. It amazed him how instantly he'd fallen in love with her. He'd only known her for a few seconds when he realized he would give his life for hers without a moment's thought.

Having Abigail made him miss his parents. He wished they could see this lovely baby that had come down through their family tree. Holding her made him wonder about his ancestors and think about those who would come after him. So much was wrapped up in such a tiny bundle, it was often hard for him to fathom. And harder when deep, stabbing pain kept shooting through the back of his eyes.

Abigail's eyelids fluttered, which meant she was on her way back to sleep. Maybe he wouldn't need that coffee after all. Gently swaying back and forth, he tried not to make a sound, barely breathing, as he watched her body slowly relax. Her tiny fists uncurled, and then her head fell back a little, and the next thing he knew, she was in a deep, sound sleep, oblivious to everything around her.

At the bottom of the stairs, Goose and Bunny raised their heads, seeming to feel his pain, and looking pretty exhausted themselves. Wolfe tiptoed toward the staircase, trying to ignore the flip-flop sound of his slippers, the loudest noise in the entire house at the moment. Licking his lips and trying to take in a deep breath, he slowly placed one foot in front of the other, climbing while balancing the baby in such a way that she thought she wasn't moving at all.

Almost there. Steady…

But just as he was about to reach the halfway mark on the stairs, the silence was undone by a knock at the front door. Goose and Bunny scrambled to their feet, announcing the visitor with vicious barks. They were smart dogs, and this wasn't the time of day someone would normally come calling.

"You have got to be kidding me!" Wolfe turned on the staircase and rushed downward, jiggling Abigail into a fully awake state as she bounced around in his arms. "Goose! Bunny! Hush!"

But it was useless. The dogs wouldn't stop until they saw whoever was at the door. Wolfe peered through the peephole into near darkness. He could see someone standing on his porch step. It looked like a female. He undid the locks and swung open the door. The cold hit him first, followed by Lois Stepaphanolopolis's excited voice, which made Wolfe blink like someone was throwing sand in his face.

"Hold on, hold on!" Wolfe said, raising one hand. Her stream of words came to a screeching halt. Wolfe rubbed his eyes, the left one in particular, since it had started to spasm at the thought of having to make a wakeful appearance.

"Are you okay?" Lois asked and then in a coochy-coo voice said, "Hi, baby Abigail."

"Am I okay?" Wolfe tried to focus his eyes. "Why are you asking me if I'm okay?"

Lois put her attention back on him. "Because you don't look like you're feeling well."

"In case you haven't noticed," Wolfe said with a grand gesture toward the night sky, "it's the middle of the night."

"I thought it was morning."

"Do you see the sun?"

Lois glanced around and then upward, like it was the first time she'd noticed the lack of daylight. "Well, the clock said a.m."

"Lois, is there an emergency?"

"No," she said with a smile. "An urgency, though."

"Are you certain it's urgent enough to wake us up?" Wolfe was having a hard time keeping his foul mood inside.

"Yes."

Suddenly Wolfe noticed a large envelope in Lois's hand as she held it out toward him.

"What's this?"

"Genius, all wrapped up in manila." She winked. Then she slid past him into his house. "Oh, coffee! Great!"

Wolfe sighed and shut the door. The only person who didn't seem to be having a good time at this hour was Wolfe. Abigail was kicking her feet and staring at the bright lights. Lois was chattering and helping herself to coffee. "...Dickens was a creative genius. He was before his time. Unappreciated. But that is going to stop here and now. I am going to bring *A Christmas Carol* into the light for everyone to see." She handed him a cup of coffee. "Sugar? Cream?"

Wolfe's head spun. "Uh...no..." Why was she offering him sugar and cream?

"Come on in," she said, gesturing toward the living room. "Make yourself at home."

Wolfe pressed on one of his temples. "I am home."

"That's a compliment," Lois said, obviously pleased. "I've always wanted to make people feel comfortable. Sure I can't get you anything?"

"Lois, you're making no sense."

"Aha!" Lois said. "That's what they said of Dickens! But he *does* make sense. Lots of sense. You just have to get over his poor grammar, odd use of punctuation, and apparent fondness for King James." She leaned in. "I think he might've been illiterate, but that doesn't mean he doesn't have a gift for storytelling."

Wolfe sat down. His legs couldn't carry him through this kind of conversation anymore. But with all the noise, Abigail didn't seem to mind sitting, and she turned her small head to look at Lois. Wolfe gulped his coffee. "Lois, Dickens wasn't illiterate. He wrote in a style that was indicative of the time and place in which he lived. That book was published in London in 1843."

Lois looked thoughtful. "Well, I guess that explains 'bah' and 'humbug.' The British always have had an odd relationship with words, haven't they? Gobsmacked. Codswallop. And did you know they spell gray with an *e*? Why not spell purple with a *q*?"

"Lois, as much as I would love to sit here and try to explain the phenomenon of Charles Dickens to you, I really need to get my daughter to sleep and then myself."

"Let me give you some advice. If you let those young ones nap all they want, they won't sleep at night."

"It *is* night, Lois. See? Outside? Pitch black!"

Lois shrugged and sipped her coffee, peering at him over her mug. "Fine. But don't say I didn't tell you so. Now, about Dickens—"

"Lois, I don't want to talk about Dickens right now. I want to sleep."

Lois sighed and nodded, then rose and went to the door. *Thank goodness,* Wolfe thought as he managed to get himself to a standing position again, trying to be a good host and see her out the door.

Ainsley had taught him good manners. They usually didn't come in handy, but he tried anyway. Lois opened the door. The cold air came in again. "Well, then, good night, Wolfe."

"Good night, Lois."

"We'll chat tomorrow?"

"Fine."

Lois waited, standing at the door, holding its knob like it might fall off if she let go. "Then, good night," she said.

"Yes, yes. Good night."

Lois's smile faded a little. "Well, what are you waiting for? An escort?"

"What are you talking about?"

Lois gestured out the door. "Exit's that way."

"I'm not leaving. You're leaving."

"I am?" Lois looked around, then at the coffee mug in her hand. "Oh...how embarrassing."

Which part? Lois was acting very strangely, and Wolfe's manners were out the door already. "So, off you go."

Lois nodded, still looking confused, and then walked out, leaving the door open and keeping the mug. Wolfe watched Lois walk down his porch steps. "Lois," Wolfe called, against his better judgment, "are you sure you're okay?"

Lois turned and smiled. "I'm fine."

"You're sure? You're acting very confused."

"No, no. Don't worry about me. I've just been up working."

"Maybe you need to get some sleep."

"Sleep. Bah! Sleep is overrated!"

Could've fooled him.

CHAPTER 3

> "Why did you get married?" said Scrooge.
> "Because I fell in love."
> "Because you fell in love!" growled Scrooge, as if that were the only one thing in the world more ridiculous than a merry Christmas.

WOLFE WOKE TO SOUNDS of crying, but as he pried open one eye, he noticed the room was filled with sunlight. It was already morning? He could've sworn he'd just put his head down and rolled to his side.

He could tell from Abigail's cry that she was hungry, which meant it had to be around nine. Ainsley had her on a strict schedule. She had them all on a strict schedule. Even the dogs had to be put outside at certain times to make sure they didn't wake the baby.

Wolfe sat up, willing both eyes to open. Crawling out of bed, he shuffled to the bathroom, turned on ice-cold water, and splashed it on his face.

Downstairs, he found Ainsley feeding the baby. There were dark circles under Ainsley's eyes, but she was gazing sweetly at Abigail.

"Hey," Wolfe said.

She looked up and her smile drooped. "Are you okay?"

"Why?"

"You just look...well...you look..."

"Dead?"

"Worse."

Wolfe went over to the coffee, which he knew would be cold by now. He poured a cup and drank it anyway. Ainsley picked Abigail up to burp her over her shoulder. "Bad night?"

"Weird night."

"Weird? What happened?"

"Lois came over."

"What do you mean she came over?"

"That's what I mean. In the middle of the night. To talk about Charles Dickens."

"Are you sure you weren't dreaming?"

Wolfe stared into his coffee. "No, not really. I mean, sleep deprivation can do weird things to people. Maybe I imagined the whole thing."

"Why would Lois come over in the middle of the night to talk about Charles Dickens?"

"I never found out. I asked her to leave."

"You know she sleepwalks."

"Yes. And apparently sleep stalks too."

Wolfe took Abigail, who was getting irritated because she couldn't burp. Wolfe knew if he stood, leaned forward a little, and patted her back just between the shoulder blades, she'd let a good one rip.

"Good girl." Wolfe kissed Abigail's cheek, then handed her back to Ainsley. He fell onto the couch next to them and leaned his head back. "Can you die from sleep deprivation?"

Chuckling, Ainsley went to the kitchen and started a fresh pot of coffee. "You have to snap out of it. We have a lot to do today. We're going to put up the Christmas tree, and we need to get our lights up. Do you know we're almost the last house to put up lights?"

"Huh."

"Plus, I'd like to go into town today and get Abigail a nice Christmas dress." She handed him his coffee. "Can you get Abigail dressed for me? I need to take a shower. Her clothes and a fresh diaper are over there. Remember to put the blanket under her in case she has another accident like yesterday." That had been fun. And had required them both to change clothes. "When you're finished, give her the pacifier, set the timer for ten minutes, and then take it out."

Wolfe gave her a look.

"That's what the book says. So they don't get too attached."

Wolfe was going to find that book and strategically misplace it. He watched her bound upstairs, wondering how she had the energy to bound. He barely had the energy to blink.

Ainsley seemed made for motherhood. Every aspect of it was delightful to her. Though Wolfe would never admit it to her, or anyone else for that matter, it was harder on him. It didn't come naturally. He loved his daughter with all his heart, but changing a diaper wasn't "the sweetest thing ever." Ainsley approached it like it was a minor miracle. Wolfe approached it like it was—well, a dirty diaper. There was nothing adorable about it, no matter how many ways Ainsley described it.

Abigail lay on the blanket, seemingly content. Wolfe kept his coffee on the table and knelt on the floor. "Okay," he said with a sigh. "Now, we're going to do this on the count of three."

Oliver leaned in eagerly as he listened to every word Lois said. "Uh-huh. Go on."

She talked very fast, but he thought he was catching on. At least to the important parts.

"So you're saying that I would need to be at practice three times a week? Plus weekends?"

"Yes," she answered.

He nodded. "I can do that."

"You're sure? You don't want to talk to Melb first? It's quite a commit—"

"No, no. She'll be fine with it," he said, glancing toward the kitchen where Melb was feeding Ollie Jr.

"I need total dedication to the vision, Oliver. I need to make sure you're on board, one hundred percent."

"Yes. Totally. One hundred percent. If you need me to be there five days a week, I'll be there."

Lois reclined in her chair and studied him. "You really see this, don't you?"

He nodded, though he had to admit he wasn't sure what she was talking about.

"You're catching the vision! I can see it in your eyes. Thank goodness," she sighed, "because I have to say, I've shared this with a few people, and they didn't seem to be getting it. But you get it."

"I do. You were saying something about late-night rehearsals, right? That's a sure thing?"

"It's a possibility. We don't have a lot of time. I'm still trying to cast the parts. Which part are you interested in?"

"Which part has the most lines and will require me to be at every rehearsal?"

"That would be Scrooge, but—"

"Great! I'll take it."

"Oliver, no offense, but you don't really seem like you could carry the role of Scrooge."

"Bah, humbug."

"Well, that was convincing." She raised an eyebrow. "But you're going to have to frown a lot and seem heartless."

"Not a problem. I want the role."

"All right. It's yours." She leaned forward to hug him. "Thanks, Cousin."

Oliver walked her to the door. "Go get some rest. You look tired."

"To tell you the truth, I've never thought more clearly."

"Oliver?" Melb called from the kitchen. He closed the door behind Lois and walked to the kitchen. Ollie held his bottle.

"Yes, dear?"

"Is Lois still here?"

"Just left. Listen, she wants me to play the lead role in her Christmas play. I couldn't turn her down. She was practically begging me, nearly in tears. I had to say yes. There'll be some rehearsals and all that. Hope it's okay."

Melb looked at him skeptically, but then smiled. "Sure. By the way, I was thinking we might go out in the backyard today and introduce Ollie to all the different colors of leaves. I want him to feel the textures of the grass and the bark on the trees. Maybe spot a cardinal."

"Oh…uh, yeah… You know, honey, I would love to, but, um, I've got that thingy this morning."

"What thingy?"

"Oh...you know... What is that called...?"

"The community center Christmas meeting?"

"That's it!"

She wiped Ollie's face and turned to him. "You've changed."

Oliver swallowed. *Uh-oh.*

"Having a child has made you a really unselfish person. You never liked community service much before, but look at you now! Giving of your time."

"Right..." He glanced at his watch. "Well, speaking of time, I'd better be going. I'll see you in a few?" *Hours.*

"Sounds good! We'll take Ollie out later, when it's a little warmer."

Oliver nodded as he grabbed his coat, car keys, and wallet. Racing out the door, he got into his car, locked it, turned the ignition, and careened out of the driveway, hoping to escape before Melb realized the community meeting was yesterday.

Wolfe sat in the coffee shop, his hands wrapped around his coffee mug, wishing he could doze off. The three shots of espresso were doing a fine job of confusing his body signals. Part of him wanted to slip into a deep, sound sleep, while the other part of him wanted to juggle something.

At least he was out of the house for a little while.

"Well, well, you've escaped."

Wolfe looked up to find Alfred standing above him, removing his silk scarf and pulling off his expensive leather gloves. He smiled and sat in one of two free chairs at Wolfe's table. "You look like you could use some adult company."

Wolfe smiled mildly. "That bad?"

"Remember that deadline that you missed by four months? Remember how I flew to your house, we stayed up all night working on it, and finished it at eight the next morning?" Wolfe nodded. "You look like that, times ten. Maybe what you need is a good, old-fashioned shove back into your career. Give you something to do with your time, hmm?"

Wolfe shot him a look. "It's just a little harder than I thought it would be. They sleep and eat, you know? How hard can it be? Except they don't sleep."

Alfred chuckled. "Oh, now, Wolfe, cheer up. Isn't this Christmas spirit supposed to carry you from the day after Thanksgiving until the first day of the new year?"

"You're being facetious, aren't you?"

"How can people keep this up for so long? It's barely December. Everybody is getting carried away here. If I don't smile and say 'good day' to everyone I meet, they start wondering why I don't have my Christmas socks on."

Wolfe laughed. "Surely you're used to it by now. It hasn't grown on you even a little?"

"Sort of. Like an asymmetrical mole that needs the attention of a doctor."

They both spotted Oliver rushing into the coffee shop, headed straight for their table. Several expressions flashed across his face. "Hi," he said, grabbing the free chair and sitting down. "Hi."

"You okay?" Wolfe asked.

Oliver glanced at Alfred, then at Wolfe, and then, with what seemed like a great deal of labor, stretched a smile onto his face. "Yes. I'm perfectly fine. Life is more terrific than I could ever imagine it would be. I'm so happy, I'm beyond words."

Alfred groaned. "See what I mean?"

"Really?" Wolfe said. "I'm barely holding on by the skin of my teeth."

The smile dropped off Oliver's face. "You, too? Thank goodness. I thought I was the only one. It's terrible. I'm a grown man who feels like he could cry at any second. I'm exhausted. My wife has lost her mind. And a person who can't even stand up by himself has complete and utter control over every single thing in our lives. Do you know, just the other day, I was forced to eat strained spinach so Ollie would want to do what his daddy does?" Oliver looked at Wolfe. "So how'd you escape?"

"I offered to go to the store. I haven't made it there yet. You?"

"Community center Christmas meeting."

"That was yesterday."

"I know. But I can wander around for a while, asking people how I missed it. Throw up my hands when I get home and blame lack of sleep." Oliver glanced around covertly, then said, "Listen, if you want some time out of the house, I've got a way."

Wolfe leaned in. "How?"

"My cousin is putting on a Christmas production of *A Christmas Carol.* I got the lead role of Scrooge."

"She's doing *A Christmas Carol*?" Alfred asked, his tone serious.

"Yes! And we have rehearsals! Several nights a week!" Oliver rubbed his hands together. "Isn't that great?"

"Yeah…except I don't really see you as Scrooge. And you're not really into theater, are you?" Wolfe asked.

"Not at all. But I can pull off any character for a chance to get away from the house. I mean, how hard can Scrooge be? You just act spiteful and cranky." Oliver glanced at Alfred. "Like Alfred here."

Wolfe noticed that Alfred suddenly seemed in a particularly foul mood. "You okay, Alfred?"

Alfred's glowering expression faded, and he looked at Wolfe. "Fine."

"Are you sure? You seem very annoyed. More than usual."

"I'm just distracted by the little old lady whose earrings are blinking out of sync with her sweater."

"You don't like Christmas?" Oliver asked, as they studied the woman sitting with a friend. The thought seemed unfathomable to Skary residents. Wolfe had grown used to their gusto and glee over the years, and he supposed he'd become the same way. But he knew how Alfred felt. There were years in the past when Christmas came and went without so much as a pause in his life. He would look down from his house and see the town bustling with activity, but he wasn't a part of it. Not until Ainsley.

Alfred pulled on his trench coat. "Is that a crime here?"

Oliver looked to Wolfe for help. Wolfe winked at Alfred. "You never know. You might convert."

"Funny," Alfred said, swinging his scarf around his neck. "If you see me in a 'ho ho ho' sweater, it means I've gone insane." He bade farewell and was out the door.

Oliver looked at Wolfe. "I can get you in. Lois will listen to me. If you want a role, just say the word."

"No offense to your cousin, Oliver, but I'm not sure Lois really 'gets' Dickens. First of all, she thought he was an undiscovered writer. Second, tackling *A Christmas Carol*? That's a beloved story."

"She's got an out-of-the-box idea for it. She said people will never see it coming."

"What kind of idea? People don't like their beloved stories tampered with. Believe me. I tried updating 'Little Red Riding Hood' in a short story collection and got hate mail for months."

Oliver sat back in his chair and studied Wolfe. "To tell you the truth, I don't care. All I know is that I can get out of the house at least four times a week. Are you in or not?"

Wolfe weighed the options carefully. His mother had always told him never to go to bed angry, but no one ever explained what you should do if you never went to bed. Should you make a decision or wait and sleep on it? Assuming sleep might come sooner rather than later.

"All right, fine," Wolfe said. "I'm in. But I only want a small role. Make sure Lois knows that."

"I will." Oliver grabbed his coat and stood.

"Where are you going?"

"I've got to go stand in front of the community center for a few minutes."

"Why?"

"The last time I tried to escape by way of servicing our car, Melb ran into Larry, who said I hadn't been in. So this way, there are witnesses who can say I was standing there, scratching my head and looking confused about why the meeting wasn't there." He shot a meaningful glance at Wolfe. "And you'd better get to the grocery store. Trust me."

CHAPTER 4

> "They are Man's," said the Spirit, looking down upon them. "And they cling to me, appealing from their fathers. This boy is Ignorance. This girl is Want. Beware them both, and all of their degree, but most of all beware this boy, for on his brow I see that written which is Doom, unless the writing be erased."

"NO!" ALFRED SCREAMED. The little boy stared, his eyes gaping holes, his mouth open and moaning. His skin looked white and dead, and Alfred was afraid that if he peered forward, he might see maggots coming out. Nothing would be more terrifying, except seeing the devil himself.

"No!" Alfred said again, walking backward. But no matter how he moved his feet, he could only stay still. "No!"

A hand grabbed his arm, and Alfred shrieked.

"Alfred!"

"What?"

"Alfred! Snap out of it!"

The next thing he knew, he was lying flat on his own couch, staring into the eyes of someone much less terrifying. Well, not *much* less.

"Lois?"

"Are you all right?" she asked.

"Why are you in my home?" he asked, sitting up.

"I was outside knocking, and I heard you scream. Your door was unlocked, so I came in. You were dreaming, I think. Either that, or you were trying to impress me."

"Impress you?" He flew to his feet. "What do you mean by that?"

She grinned. "You want a part, don't you?"

"A part of what?"

"A part in my play."

"No, I don't want a part! Are you crazy?"

She frowned. "Why would I be crazy?"

He backed out of the room, pretending there was something in his kitchen he needed to attend to. He put the teakettle on. "Would love some, thanks," Lois said, trailing behind him. She parked herself on the stool at the breakfast bar. "To tell you the truth, I wanted you to play Scrooge, but the part's already taken. People are scrambling as fast as they can to get a role. Wolfe just called me to see about it."

"Then why do you need me?" Alfred asked, keeping his back to her. "Obviously, you have enough actors."

"Yes, but are they the right ones? I want the right ones. I've been thinking this over, and I think I would like you to play the Ghost of Christmas Present."

"No!" He turned and fixed his eyes on her. "No. Absolutely not."

"Is it too big of a role?"

"I just don't want to be involved. Period." Lois was about to say something, but he cut her off. "Cast Wolfe. He's perfect for that role. You know he's going to tell you he just wants a small role, but on the inside, Wolfe really likes acting, and he's just too humble to ask for the bigger roles. Insist that he take it, okay?"

Lois seemed to be thinking about it. "I suppose he would be good in that role. The bags under his eyes will work for him, in this case." She stood. "I would love to chat, but I really should go. I've got to talk to Marlee, see if she wants the role."

"For what? Mrs. Cratchit?"

She tilted her head. "Mrs. Cratchit? Of course not. She's all wrong for that. I'm going to cast her as Marley."

"Jacob Marley?"

"Yes."

"Jacob Marley is male…"

"I took her name as a sign that the role should be hers. You should learn to read signs better, Alfred."

"Jacob Marley is an old, penny-pinching miser, just like Scrooge."

"I know," Lois said, her voice lowering as a mischievous twinkle gleamed in her eyes. "That's what everyone is expecting, right? In case you haven't noticed, Alfred, I don't like the status quo. There's nothing wrong with stirring things up a little. Besides, come on. Really. How many people have actually read the book?"

"Everybody I know."

She chuckled. "Overstating things, as usual. I guess that's what made you good at whatever it was you used to do. I'll be going now, but think about it, will you?"

Alfred watched her trot down the porch steps, and he shut the door just as the teakettle whistled.

His mind wandered back to his dream. He hadn't dreamed about it in years, but it was no wonder he was doing it now. "Calm down," he told himself. He could still see the boy's face in his mind.

He wasn't sure if it would ever go away, not as long as *A Christmas Carol* was still around. And since it had been around for more than a hundred and fifty years, it probably wasn't going anywhere soon.

Pouring his tea, he wondered what had happened to Susie Perry. She'd played Want. Alfred thought she was the cutest eight-year-old he'd ever seen. Her hay-colored hair fell in long ringlets down her back, and her eyes twinkled blue, no matter what kind of light she stood in. When she smiled, deep dimples creased both cheeks. It was hard getting her to look ugly, as the role of Want dictated. Much harder than it was to make Alfred look that way.

They'd rehearsed together as Ignorance and Want for weeks, and with each passing day, he fell more and more head-over-heels. Susie seemed to like him too. And since they only appeared once in the entire play, they had a lot of time to talk. She liked marbles and pick-up sticks. They spent some of their time playing dice games behind the theater building.

One day while they squatted near each other, rolling the dice, Alfred got up the nerve to kiss her. For a solid thirty minutes, he had slowly inched closer to her. Biting his lip, he watched her roll the dice and giggle with delight as two sixes came up.

Squeezing his eyes and puckering his lips, he leaned in, his lips brushing up against her soft cheek.

"Alfred Tennison!" she exclaimed. "What in the world are you doing?"

Alfred opened his eyes, expecting to see a smile, but there wasn't one.

"Oh…um…" Did he really need to *explain* what he was doing? "It's just…well, Susie, I like you. I hope you like me. I really like you."

Susie's eyes widened, just like they did in the play when she was supposed to look scary. "Don't say such a thing!"

"Why not?" Alfred asked.

She put her hands on her hips. "I'm in love with Jonathan."

"Tiny Tim?" Alfred could hardly believe what he was hearing. "He's half your size! And walks with a limp!" Jonathan Swaim was cast as Tiny Tim mostly because he was, indeed, tiny. His eyes were naturally sunken, and his skin was pale because his mother would never let him go outside to play.

"He's cute," Susie said.

"What about me?"

"I don't know," Susie said earnestly. "I mean, you can look very scary."

"I'm *acting.*"

"I know," she said, looking overwhelmed by the moment. "But my mama always told me to stay away from ignorant boys."

"I'm not ignorant! I play the character Ignorance." Susie just blinked at him and shrugged. "What about Tiny Tim? He's about to die, you know."

"That's just pretend."

"You're not making any sense," young Alfred insisted.

Susie set her shoulders square. "I like him. I don't like you. Does that make better sense?"

He nodded, staring at the dice on the ground. He hated playing Ignorance. He'd played that role since he was six. His father was a theater director and for two years had cast his son as Ignorance. Truthfully, Alfred really wanted to play Tiny Tim, but he'd overheard his parents conversing about it one night. His dad said that he just didn't fit the part. He wasn't likable enough. Tiny Tim had to be likable. So instead, he got to play a character described as wretched, abject, frightful, hideous, miserable. Yellow, meager, ragged, scowling. Wolfish. Yes, wolfish. And if that wasn't enough, Dickens went further: *No change, no degradation, no perversion of humanity, in any grade, through all the mysteries of wonderful creation, has monsters half so horrible and dread.*

That'll win the ladies.

And apparently he'd played the part quite well. When he'd peeked out from under the spirit's robe, the audience had gasped, recoiled, put their hands over their mouths. One woman cried.

Eventually he rebelled and refused to do the role, but he never outgrew his disdain for Charles Dickens and his horrible story. Perhaps it wasn't fair to completely blame Charles Dickens for his insolence toward Christmas. After all, Alfred's parents could certainly share in the blame. They did Christmas the way you did Christmas if you wanted Chevy Chase to star in the movie made about your life. Except his life wouldn't have been nearly as exciting. The cranky aunts showed up every year, his parents complained about money, his uncles got drunk, and he never got a single thing he asked for. Throughout his childhood, all the way until he turned sixteen, Alfred thought Christmas might, just might, turn out like that movie *A Christmas Story.* He would lie awake at night, dreaming of his father, with a kindling excitement in his eyes, watching his son tear open a last package, then look disappointed. His father would then exclaim, "Wait! What is this? One more package hidden behind the couch!"

But no. That excitement was actually for the gifts under the tree, ranging from a set of encyclopedias to an ant farm, which was particularly strange since Alfred, at the age of two, had developed a horrible phobia of bugs.

Steeping his teabag, he wondered if it might not be better just to return to New York for the holidays.

Then he heard it. No, it couldn't be. It was his imagination. He listened. He looked at his television, but it was off. Slowly, cautiously, he tiptoed toward his door, and sure enough, the sound got louder. And louder. And louder. He flung open the door and scowled at the eight women and two men who were about to sing of french hens but instead gasped.

"What are you doing?" Alfred yelled.

One small woman said, "We're singing."

"Why?"

"Christmas caroling," another woman said. Each held a black book, opened and lying flat in their hands. Though it wasn't nearly cold enough, each had donned either a stocking cap or earmuffs. All had matching red gloves.

They were just about to kick into another stanza when Alfred held his hand up. "I don't want you to sing here."

"But—"

"No! No! Go away! Scram!" That usually worked for all the cats around, and if he'd had a broom nearby, he would've used it.

One woman's mouth dropped open, some whispered as they backed away, and still others turned and stomped off.

"It's December fifth!" Alfred called after them. "The *fifth*! The FIFTH!" He stepped back inside and slammed the door.

This was going to be a very long month.

Dr. Hass sat in his chair, his fingertips forming a steeple as he peered over his glasses at Alfred. Alfred clutched the flier left in his door a few weeks ago, offering counseling at a buy-two-get-one-free rate from the man who prided himself on being "practically relevant" but, in fine print, not actually a psychologist in the conventional way. It certainly was no surprise to Alfred that the town shrink was as weird as the rest of the people, but he was desperate for relief... and some answers.

He was hoping for something like hypnosis. He'd once heard you could cure smoking with it. Maybe it would work with haunting dreams.

"How long have you had these dreams?"

"They come and go," Alfred answered. "But more recently, they've been coming frequently. Making matters worse is the fact that Lois Stepaphanolopolis is doing the play. She keeps insisting I need a role."

"What did you tell her?"

"No. Absolutely not."

"Alfred, how long did you play the character of Ignorance?"

"Long enough, until one day, in the middle of dress rehearsal, I stomped off the stage and told my father I would never play the role again!"

Dr. Hass leaned forward. "I bet you felt a lot of guilt for doing that."

"My parents made sure of it."

"Perhaps these dreams would go away if you did indeed participate in the play?"

Alfred frowned. "Isn't that giving in?"

"Maybe, but it's also like sticking your tongue out at your folks and telling them you'll be in the play when you're good and ready."

"Tell me something, Dr. Hass," Alfred began, ignoring the pseudoshrink's questionable advice. "Tell me why Wolfe Boone seems to be perfectly content."

"I don't understand."

"We're both in the same predicament, the way I see it. We're both out of work, for the most part, and can't seem to resurrect our careers to the place they used to be. We don't really do anything else well, so getting another job is out of the question. But..."

"Yes?"

"He seems happy."

"Well, Alfred, people can seem happy, even when they're not."

"I don't know. I mean, the guy used to be kind of brooding, you know? And not in an 'I want to be noticed' sort of way. He really was brooding. All the time. I hardly ever saw him smile. He's different now. It's like everything is enjoyable to him."

"Is he working on a new book?"

"Every time I ask him that, he tells me he's writing an unauthorized biography about me."

Dr. Hass laughed, but Alfred didn't.

"Anyway, I guess I just want to know why he's content and I'm not. And don't tell me it's the wife and baby, because he's got a case of the nags and the bags," Alfred said, pointing to underneath his eye, "and I wouldn't want any of that."

"Alfred, I think the reason for your discontentment is clear."

Alfred leaned forward and engaged Dr. Hass. "Yes? What is it?"

"You haven't put up your Christmas lights yet!"

Chapter 5

"Merry Christmas! What right have you to be merry? What reason have you to be merry? You're poor enough."

"Come, then," returned the nephew gaily. "What right have you to be dismal? What reason have you to be morose? You're rich enough."

WOLFE SPOONED turkey delight into Abigail's mouth as quickly as he could. The smell nauseated him. Wolfe wondered why he couldn't feed her the apple cobbler, but Ainsley wouldn't hear anything about it. "If you feed her the sweet stuff, that's all she's going to want to eat." Even the sweet potato purée was off limits, except on Saturdays. He watched Ainsley cleaning the dishes and thought through his plan as he studied his daughter's face. She was the spitting image of Ainsley, except she'd inherited Wolfe's slightly crooked ears. Her hair was white-blond, and her eyes perfectly round like she was in a perpetual state of excitement. Scooping the dribble off her chin, he decided she was getting a little full. Maybe she wasn't, but he had to get some fresh air.

"Hey," he said, leaning on the counter next to Ainsley. "Something's come up that I wanted to run past you."

"What?"

"Lois is putting on a Christmas play."

Ainsley turned with surprise. "Really? I love Christmas plays!"

That's going to help.

"It's quite a large cast, and Lois is looking for actors."

"Okay..."

"It's *A Christmas Carol*," he added quickly.

"Oooo! I love the classics! And that's my favorite of Charles Dickens!"

"It *is* wonderful." Wolfe glanced back at Abigail. She was chewing on her bib. "Lois wants me to be in it."

"Wolfe, don't you remember what happened the last time you were in one of Lois's plays? You swore you wouldn't do another."

"I know," Wolfe said, trying to think fast on his feet. "But it is one of our favorites. And I'd get to play one of the ghosts."

Ainsley set down the dish she was drying and turned to him. "I don't know, Wolfe. Last time, you were completely stressed out. Grumpy all the time. And if I remember correctly, you and Lois have very different artistic tastes."

"She's desperate. You should've seen her. Nearly in tears. I don't want to disappoint her."

"But it's so close to Christmas as it is. She's just now starting?"

"You can see why she's desperate."

"Well, what's the rehearsal schedule like?"

He'd known that question was coming. He hoped he'd buttered her up enough, but in reality, she wasn't looking very buttery. "As you pointed out, we don't have a lot of time, so I'll be gone a couple or five nights a week."

A small, disappointed frown appeared.

"But I'm home during the days," he added. "All day. Mornings and throughout the night..."

Ainsley glanced at Abigail, and then back at Wolfe. "I don't know..."

"Oliver gets to do it." And he sounded exactly like a third grader when he said it, too.

Ainsley bit her lip, thinking it over.

He was nearly to the point of dropping to his knees and pleading when she said, "Wolfe, I know the last few weeks have been really hard. We're both exhausted. And I know you need to get out of the house."

Wolfe stood there, not sure whether he should be nodding enthusiastically or disagreeing emphatically.

Then she blinked slowly, smiled, and rested her hand on his arm. "Of course you can, honey. It sounds fun."

Alfred stepped out the door of Dr. Hass's office and right into the path of Sheriff Parker, who took a firm stance and gave him a hard look.

"Sheriff," Alfred said in a polite tone that would've gone nicely with a hat-tipping, if he'd been wearing one.

"Alfred." The sheriff didn't tip his hat, and he was wearing one. "What seems to be the problem?"

"Problem?" He *was* coming out of Dr. Hass's office, but most of the time when people wanted to know your business, they used the indirect approach and asked a neighbor.

"I got a report this morning," the sheriff said.

"A report about what?"

"Christmas carolers? Harassing? Ring a bell?"

"Yes! And thank you for taking it seriously. It was infuriating, and I'm not going to put up with it any longer. There should be some sort of ordinance or city code or something. I know we'll never be able to get rid of them completely, but maybe they should only be allowed to do it starting December twenty-third."

The sheriff crossed his arms. "You got something against Christmas carolers?"

Uh-oh. "They filed a report on me?"

"Harassment is a very serious violation in our town, Mr. Tennison."

"I wasn't harassing them! They were harassing me!"

"If this is any indication, no wonder they were frightened."

"Frightened? I asked them to leave my property."

"First of all, it's not your property. You rent it from Mr. Duvane. Secondly, we don't shout. And we certainly don't shout at elderly people who are trying to bring some Christmas cheer."

"Look, this is a huge misunderstanding," Alfred said. "It all started when I woke up to the sound of Lo—" Alfred caught himself. Lois was the sheriff's girlfriend, or fiancée, or something. Best to avoid this.

"The sound of what?"

"The point is that I wasn't prepared for it."

"That's obvious. You haven't even hung Christmas lights."

"I have a bad back."

"Mr. Johanson is in a wheelchair, and he managed to get his lights up."

"Of course he did."

The sheriff placed his hands on his hips. Well, one hip and a gun holster. Then he pulled a pad of paper out of his pocket.

"Are you writing me a ticket?"

"Yep."

"For what?"

"You know what."

"That's a crime?"

"That's for the court to decide. You'll have to make an appearance at the county courthouse, which is forty-seven miles east and usually very crowded and running behind." The sheriff continued writing. "The penalty will most likely be community service." He glanced up at Alfred. "Of course, we could just cut to the chase and get that over with now."

Alfred propped his own hands on his hips. "What did you have in mind? Picking up trash on the side of the road?"

"Your buddy Hass here's got that covered from his fiasco a few months back. But there is something..."

"What?"

"The community is putting on a Christmas play. It's not called 'community theater' for nothing. The community usually gets involved."

Alfred started to get that sinking feeling, the same one that came when he got word that one of Wolfe's books was going to be reviewed by some highbrow literary magazine.

"What are you suggesting?"

The sheriff looked down at the ticket he'd just torn from the pad. "We can skip all the paperwork."

Alfred slumped. "What do you want me to do?"

"Don't ask me. Ask Lois. She's at the theater right now." He glanced up at the sign over Dr. Hass's office. "And you didn't ask me, but if it helps, staying busy is the best cure for the blues."

Lois had always thought of herself as an especially tolerant person. She didn't scowl at the people who felt the need to "amen" during the sermons, she didn't gripe to her neighbors about where they put their outdoor trash cans, she didn't curse at slow lines or raise Cain about taxes. But the one thing she just couldn't seem to dismiss was the know-it-all.

And here he was, sitting on *her* stage, treating her like she was an idiot.

"You're just being small minded, Wolfe," Lois interrupted. "Yes, I realize Jacob Marley is supposed to be a man. But I'm updating the story. In case you haven't noticed, that's been done to a classic or two."

Wolfe sighed loudly. "I know that. But making Jacob Marley into Jae Cobb-Marley, a ruthless businesswoman in the fashion industry who is only interested in herself, doesn't really fit the pulse of the story. You have to understand that Dickens wrote this in the mid-1800s in England. The poverty, filth, and disease that the people had to endure at that time were unimaginable. It's been said that nearly half of the funerals then were for children, which is why the passage that Dickens wrote when the Ghost of Christmas Yet To Come shows Scrooge the death of Tiny Tim was particularly moving. Many people had lost a child themselves."

"I have Tiny Tim in the play, Wolfe. And all the other characters. I'm bringing some of them into modern times, but it's not like I'm rewriting the story."

"Some of the characters?"

"Much of the appeal of the story is that it takes people back to a time that isn't ours. But why not mix it up with some characters from our time? A bridge-the-gap sort of thing."

Wolfe tried not to wince. "Okay, look, let's start with how you became inspired to do this particular project. Out of the entire collection of classics, what made you choose this one?"

"Oh, I just love those little porcelain Christmas villages people have sitting around their house this time of year! The nineteenth century was so pure and simple and romantic!"

"And there's the irony. It wasn't pure or simple or romantic. It was a world full of hurting people, just like now."

"Believe me, Wolfe. The message will come through loud and clear. I promise."

"But why not just cast Jacob Marley as a man? That's one of my favorite passages, where Scrooge is beholding his old business partner. Marley's jaw is hanging on its hinge, wrapped up in bandages. It's gruesome, horrific, to see him walking around, looking as if he's rotting right there in front of Scrooge. It should be appalling. Cast Marlee as Belle. She'd be perfect for Belle."

Beholding. Nice. If that's the kind of word Wolfe liked to use in his books, no wonder they were tanking. "Believe me," Lois said, not to be deterred, "I will have no problem bringing the audience to repulsion. Jae will be wearing polyester, and though you may not get it, believe me, a lot of women in the audience are going to be appalled."

Wolfe scowled.

"You're too good for this? Is that what you're saying? Too good for my little production?" Lois folded her arms. "In that case, you're welcome to go home to your family. But when it's eight-thirty at night and you're changing your tenth diaper of the day, don't come crying to me. I gave you a way out."

Wolfe's fingers traced his eyebrows. "Fine. Which ghost do you want me to play?"

"That's the kind of attitude I'm looking for. And don't get too attached to the word *ghost.* There's a good chance I might be using the word *goblin.*"

CHAPTER 6

> To say that he was not startled, or that his blood was not conscious of a terrible sensation to which it had been a stranger from infancy, would be untrue.

THIS WAS A NEW sensation, if it could be called a sensation. It was actually an antisensation. Alfred felt numb from the top of his head to the bottom of his feet. His skin was numb, his nose was numb, his brain was numb, not to mention his emotions. Or lack of emotions. He couldn't feel a thing.

Well, that wasn't exactly true. There was still fear, and he supposed that's what kept him chained to the sidewalk outside the theater. He couldn't make himself go in. Part of him scolded himself for being such a pansy and letting the sheriff—who had nothing better to do with his time—bully him into doing something for the community. But another part of him felt it might be time to face his demons. If he got involved with the play, maybe these nightmares would stop, and he could finally get over Want, Ignorance, and that rotten little pipsqueak, Tiny Tim.

"Alfred," he said quietly to himself, "you can do this. One foot in front of the other. You're strong. You're normal. You're not going to be ruled by Ignorance any more!" Alfred took one small step. "Ha! Take that, Chuck!" Another step. "Good riddance, Dickens!" Slowly, methodically, he kept taking steps forward, and with each step a nearly indescribable confidence built inside him. He even smiled and picked up his pace a little bit. He was no coward! He could do this. He could put this to rest once and for all!

"Yes, indeed!" Alfred said, swinging his arms by his side as he began a brisk walk. He arrived at the doors to the theater and, without even a hint of hesitation, reached for the handle. But before he could grab it, it swung away from his grasp. He stumbled backward, only to find Wolfe hurrying out. Wolfe's eyes grew wide when he noticed Alfred.

"What are you doing here?" Wolfe asked.

"I'm...I'm...the play."

"You're kidding."

Alfred wasn't sure. Maybe he should be, by the look on Wolfe's face. He'd seen that look before, only once, when Alfred had to break the news that the cover of one of his books had a typo in the title. They recalled all of them, but not before the late-night talk shows got wind of it.

Wolfe stepped closer, looking this way and that, until he was looking at Alfred, square in the face. "Listen to me, Alfred. I'm serious. If you never listen to me again, that's fine, but listen to me now."

"What?"

"Run for your life."

"Run?"

"Haul yourself out of here. Believe me, this is nothing you want to be involved with."

"The play?"

"Yes, the play. If you even want to call it that. I don't think that's an appropriate word. Atrocity. Yes, that's a good name."

"What's wrong?"

"What isn't wrong, that's the question." Alfred couldn't remember ever seeing Wolfe so intense. "Slaughtered."

"Someone's been slaughtered?"

"Yes. Try Marley, the three ghosts, the entire premise of the book. And that's not to mention the language, content, and spirit of the work."

Alfred just stood there, blinking.

"She's destroying a masterpiece! There's got to be some law against this."

"If there's a law about putting up Christmas lights, there might be hope for you."

Wolfe grabbed Alfred by the shoulders. "Do yourself a favor. Don't get involved in this. You'll thank me for it."

"So you're not doing it?"

Wolfe looked away sheepishly. "I'm desperate."

Alfred watched him walk away down the sidewalk, then Alfred turned his attention back to the theater. Well, he was desperate too. Not in a dirty-diaper sort of way, but in a save-the-sanity sort of way. Taking a deep breath, he flung the door open and walked inside. Really...how bad could it be?

He found Lois sitting in the middle of the stage on a folding chair, going through what looked like a script, scribbling on one page after another. She didn't hear him come in, so he waited a little bit, trying to get his courage back. Finally he stepped out of the shadows and down the aisle that led to the stage.

Lois looked up, squinting in the stage lights. "Who's there?"

"Alfred. Tennison."

He walked toward her as she put her script down. Once he was near the stage, he offered a smile. "Looks like you're working hard."

She straightened her posture and snubbed her nose a little. "Why do you care?"

"Look," Alfred said, his arms open in an apologetic, explanatory gesture. "I wanted to come to say I'm sorry about this morning. I shouldn't have yelled at you."

Lois's expression took on a little less hostility. "Go on."

"Um, well, that's what I wanted to say, and to see if you might consider me for one of the roles. I realize you've probably cast the main characters," he said, trying not to sound hopeful, "but perhaps I could take a smaller role? And by smaller, I don't mean one of the children. Just something with a few lines." He felt relief wash over him. There. He'd done it. That wasn't so bad.

But Lois didn't look convinced. "I want people who want to be here, Alfred. This is going to take a lot of time and dedication, and if you're not willing, there's no reason to be in it."

"I'm willing," he said with a placating grin. "Very willing. Enthusiastic, or as they say in your part of the world, gung-ho." They also used it in China to mean a communist organization, but that was beside the point. Thanks to the marines in World War II, who adopted it as a phrase to mean overly zealous, it had become to the English language what "aw, shucks" had become to the English gesture. But nobody in Skary, Indiana, had much use for that kind of information.

She sighed. "I don't think so, Alfred. I'm sorry. You're just not what I'm looking for."

He raised his eyebrows. "Not what you're looking for? Just a few hours ago, you were standing over me in my own house begging me to be Scrooge."

"That was then. This is now."

"How can you change your mind that quickly?"

"I'm a woman. And I have intuition. Something tells me there's more to this story. I know a thing or two about men, and one of their strong points isn't apologies."

Alfred bit his lip. Now what?

"Okay…look, maybe I can help in another way."

"Alfred, please. Don't beg. It's pitiful."

"Do you have a marketing plan?"

Lois's head popped up. "What do you mean?"

"You want to fill this theater, don't you?"

"Of course."

"How are you going to get the word out?"

"Fliers."

"To the other counties?" Alfred could see the wheels in her mind turning, so he seized the moment. "Think big, Lois. Think very big. See the potential. We get the word out to neighboring towns, and you might have yourself quite a crowd. You might even have to add a couple of matinees."

An enthusiastic smile emerged. "I hadn't thought of that."

"I could be your marketing director. With a few clever tag lines, I think you'll be turning people away at the door." Her eyes were growing wider with each word. "It's my sweet spot, Lois. I do it, and I do it well. Do you want my services or not?"

She nodded, almost as if in a trance.

"Terrific. Then you'll agree to my proposal. I get forty percent of the ticket sales for every ticket I sell above a hundred."

"A hundred?" Lois gasped. "Impossible."

"Watch and learn."

Lois licked her lips. "Deal."

"I'll get to work on it immediately. And Lois, let's keep this between you and me. I don't want people to start begging me to do marketing for them, and you do want people to believe they're coming only because of the sheer genius of your work."

Lois nodded again, and he turned to walk out the doors. Maybe it was community work, but Alfred Tennison never, ever, worked for free.

"All right, everyone, let's gather around." Lois beckoned them onto the stage. Wolfe trailed behind Oliver, hardly able to lift one foot after another. He'd read everything Dickens had written. In a sense, he felt like a traitor to be involved in such a mess as this.

A circle of chairs sat in the center of the stage. Everyone in the cast began taking their seats. Wolfe sat next to Oliver, who glanced at him with bloodshot eyes.

"I feel how you look."

"I'm afraid I won't be able to concentrate onstage. And every time I try to read something, the words go blurry, and I think I nod off sometimes."

"Maybe during breaks we can catch a nap."

"A nap…" Oliver looked like he could burst into tears. "I would pay three hundred dollars for a three-hour nap."

"Yeah, and no diaper duty for an entire day."

"You're not kidding. Two nights ago, that thing stank so bad, my eyes were watering. I was gasping for breath. I thought I might pass out."

"If you tear a Kleenex in two and stuff each half up a nostril, that usually works."

"Good tip. Thanks."

"Business going okay at the car lot?"

"Selling a lot of minivans."

"Why?"

"Because now I understand why they're such a dream car." He smiled. "If they could just make a baby carrier that didn't weigh a ton. But nothing beats sliding that door back and sticking the kid in without lifting."

Wolfe smiled. He understood. They'd bought one from Oliver in a nice forest green color.

"Attention everyone. Let's settle down. We have a lot to cover in a short period of time." Lois walked to the center of the circle and turned as she addressed everyone. "Welcome to *A Very Skary Christmas Carol.*"

"You got that right," Wolfe mumbled.

"Many of you may not be familiar with Charles Dickens. He was a little-known writer of the nineteenth century. A doctorate in English is required to understand a thing he's saying. In fact, that's where the phrase, 'What the dickens are you talking about?' came from."

Wolfe groaned. Lois glanced sideways at him but went on.

"Let me tell you the premise of the story. It revolves around three ghosts who feel the need to come back to earth to stir up trouble."

"What?" Wolfe's jaw dropped. "Lois, the story isn't about the three ghosts. It's about Scrooge."

"I'll get to Ebenezer in a moment, Wolfe. Don't get ahead of me."

"Who is Ebenezer?" Marlee asked.

Wolfe rolled his eyes. This was painful. "Ebenezer," Lois explained, "is the victim in this story."

A few eyebrows popped up. Lois didn't seem to notice or care. "So basically the three ghosts torment Scrooge until he gives them all his money."

"Lois!" Wolfe exclaimed. "You're missing the entire point of the book! The three ghosts are sent to show Scrooge how money has ruined him, and what lies ahead if he doesn't change his penny-pinching ways."

Lois clasped her hands in front of her and stared mildly at Wolfe. "Isn't that the wonderful aspect of literature, Wolfe? That it's open for interpretation?"

"You're not interpreting it. You're completely rewriting it!"

Lois gave a knowing glance to everyone else. "It's a common problem among writers," she said smoothly. "They always think their methods are the best. Wolfe, you interpret it one way. I interpret it another. I happen to believe it's a satire."

"A *satire*?"

"Showing how the government can con you into giving them all your money by making you feel sorry for people."

Wolfe stared at the floor, his head pounding and his eyes stinging from fatigue. This was getting worse by the second. But couldn't he just let it go? After all, this was Skary. Fifty people might show up for the production. And it got him out of the house for a little while, the importance of which couldn't be stated enough. Wolfe sat silently, trying to focus on Abigail's bout with the stomach flu last week as incentive to stay involved with the play.

"Now," Lois said, rubbing her hands together, "here's the twist..."

A twist? Wolfe could hardly bear to hear it.

"We're going to do this as a horror piece." Lois held up her hand at Wolfe, apparently expecting the rebuttal well on its way to spewing out. "It's a perfect fit," she said defiantly. "If you ask me, I think Dickens didn't play it up enough. Sure, he called it his little ghost story, but I'm thinking something along the lines of chain saws, hockey masks, the IRS. That's what we're going to offer our audience. A really frightening story."

"No kidding," Wolfe muttered under his breath.

"Now," she said, "let me announce the cast to you. Oliver, my favorite cousin, is going to be playing Ebenezer Scrooge. I thought he would be perfect for the role because it's easy to feel sorry for Oliver in real life, so I figured the audience would connect with him on the stage too."

Oliver cleared his throat. "Oh, um, thanks."

"Jae Cobb-Marley, Scrooge's business partner, will be played by our own Marlee Hampton. You can guess why she got the part. No, it's not only her name," Lois said with a wink. "She exudes a businesslike prowess that I'm hoping to draw out from the character." Marlee smiled, popped her shoulders up, and waved just like a businesswoman wouldn't. "Bob Cratchit is going to be played by Martin Blarty, and Willem over here is going to play Tiny Tim." Martin's warm smile had the elder Cratchit written all over it. However, Willem's smile, mischievous at best, didn't really lend itself to the boy who finally touches Scrooge's heart.

"Now for the goblins." Lois rubbed her hands together. "The

Goblin of Christmas Past." She pointed toward the sheriff and beamed. "Isn't he perfect for it?"

Wolfe, realizing he should tread lightly since the sheriff was his father-in-law and Lois's boyfriend, said nothing. The sheriff smiled a little, and Wolfe could only guess he was in this play because Lois had guilted him into it.

"The Goblin of Christmas Present, our own Garth Twyne." The town vet, who was still bitter about losing Ainsley to Wolfe, stood.

"Thank you, Lois. I would like to take this opportunity to thank—"

"Get over yourself," Lois piped in. "If it's not in your lines, we don't have time to hear it. Next, we have the Ghost of Christmas Yet To Come, Wolfe Boone." She didn't gesture or say it with any zeal, but the others clapped enthusiastically anyway.

"I'm not a goblin?"

"I'm not settled on any titles, Wolfe. It may be ghost, it may be goblin. We'll have to see what works."

"Dickens used the word 'phantom' to describe the spirit," Wolfe replied as he stood and took a little bow. If there was any role to take, this was the one. He didn't have so much as a line and would only point here and there. The applause continued, so Wolfe played up a slight British accent and quoted Dickens like a true storyteller. *"The Phantom slowly, gravely, silently, approached. When it came near him, Scrooge bent down upon his knee; for in the very air through which this Spirit moved, it seemed to scatter gloom and mystery."* *An apt description of Lois as well,* Wolfe thought. *"It was shrouded in a deep black garment, which concealed its head, its face, its form, and left nothing of it visible save one outstretched hand—"*

"Fine, fine, so he can quote Shakespeare. Stop showing off, Wolfe. And the more I think about it, the more I'm liking ghost." She pointed to Dustin. "Last but not least is Fred, Scrooge's nephew, played by Dustin."

Dustin's hands shot into the air like he was at a rock concert. "Dude, this is going to be awesome! Do I get to wear vampire teeth?"

CHAPTER 7

"Who are you?"
"Ask me who I was."
"Who were you then?"

AINSLEY AND MELB walked side by side, each pushing a stroller, both with diaper bags slung over their shoulders.

Melb stopped. "Do you think it's too cold? It seems too cold." She rushed around to the front, tugging at the stocking cap on Ollie's head. "I don't want him to get an ear infection. Oh no!"

"What?" Ainsley asked, rushing to Melb's side.

"Is that… It is!"

"What?"

"Snot!" Melb plunged her hand into her diaper bag. It re-emerged with a tissue. She pinched Ollie's nose, trying to wipe it all off. "It's clear, so that's a good sign. Yellow or green, bad news. Means an infection. Hold on…" Melb looked at her watch while placing her hand on Ollie's chest. "Okay, his breathing is normal."

Melb stood upright and took a deep breath. Ainsley put a hand on her shoulder. "Melb, it's going to be fine. Look at him. He's happy to be out and about in some fresh air. It's a little crisp out here, but nothing dreadful. We can all use some fresh air."

"I suppose," Melb said. She pointed to Ainsley's stroller. "You should remove those cup holders on the handle."

Ainsley glanced to where her warm cup of hot chocolate she got from the coffee shop sat. "Why?"

"If you hit a bump or the stroller got knocked, that hot drink could tip and spill all over Abigail, scalding her."

"Oh, uh..."

"You should subscribe to one of those parenting magazines. They've got all kinds of interesting articles. This month there's a little arts and crafts section on how to make puppets out of leftovers. It only lasts for a day because then you've got the mold to deal with, but you should see how Ollie's eyes light up when I do the little voices. The little girl had spaghetti for hair. So cute." Melb stuck her hand in the air. "We should go. I just felt a breeze."

"Melb, the kids are fine. You worry too much."

"Worry too much? Ainsley, these children are helpless. They are depending on us to make every single decision for them, from what they eat to how long they sleep. Did you know that as early as three months old, you could permanently scar your child by letting him see a troubled expression on your face? That could carry all the way to college! Have you started saving for her college, Ainsley? I realize Wolfe is out of work and all, but if I did the calculations right, adding in inflation, it will cost three hundred million dollars and eighty-two cents."

Ainsley tried not to laugh. Poor Melb. If ever there was an overly protective mother, Melb was it. Since the day Ollie was born, she had been fussing over every small detail, from the texture of the creamed peas ("He could have an aversion to vegetables for the rest of his life!") to the shape of the pacifier ("If he's going to have an oral fixation, it can't resemble his thumb") to the firmness of the mattress ("Back problems start at birth"). Ainsley supposed she couldn't talk much. She sometimes tiptoed into the nursery to make sure Abigail was still breathing. But Melb seemed to take it a step further.

"Melb," Ainsley said, guiding her toward the park bench by the sidewalk, "come sit by me."

Melb steered the stroller so it sat right next to the bench. "Maybe if he doesn't face the wind." She looked at Ainsley. "Aren't you going to get Abigail?"

"She's fine. I want to talk to you."

"About what?"

She gently placed a hand on Melb's knee. "Melb, I feel like you're missing out on the joy of being a mom."

"I'm happy. I'm very happy," Melb declared. "And if I feel like I want to curl up in the fetal position and cry myself to sleep, I make sure Ollie is out of the room. I'm afraid if he sees me in the fetal position, he's not going to want to learn to walk."

Ainsley shook her head. Melb, as usual, had missed the point. "You're a great mother. You take care of him, feed him, dress him, and most importantly, love him. But you worry. All the time. About everything. Things that most likely will never hap—"

"Aha! *Most likely.* Remember last year when that baby got his head stuck between the crib rails, and it took the fire department over an hour to free him? I bet those parents were thinking, 'It'll never happen to me.' But it *can* happen. Which is why I measured Ollie's head and then measured the spaces between the crib rails. He's fine, thank goodness, and thank the Stepaphanolopolis family for the big heads they've passed down the pipeline."

"All I'm saying is that here we are, on a beautiful winter afternoon, with the bright sun and the leaves still falling off the trees, and you're missing it because you're worried."

Melb glanced at Ollie and then sighed, slumping against the park bench and crossing her arms. "That's my job. I have to take care of him."

"You are taking care of him. He's a happy, healthy baby. And so adorable."

That made Melb smile. "He does have my looks, doesn't he?"

"Those beautiful eyes of yours...the spitting image. And Oliver's nose—"

"We'll have to wait and see on the nose. Sure, it's cutely out of proportion now, but when he hits his teens, that thing could balloon up and block his sinuses, not to mention his self-esteem."

"See? You're doing it. Projecting things into the future. He's just a baby. Live in the moment. Enjoy this time, Melb. It will go by quickly, and the next thing we know, they'll be grown."

Melb was silent for a bit, which meant that, quite possibly, Ainsley had gotten through to her. She studied Ollie, adoration in her eyes, then reached out and blotted his nose. He laughed and his entire face lit up as he looked at his mom. Suddenly, tears ran down her cheeks.

"Oh, Melb, don't cry," Ainsley said, reaching out for her.

"No, it's okay," she said, catching her tears with a finger. "It's what I needed to hear. You're right. I'm overreacting. To everything."

"You're a good mom. Don't ever doubt that. Ollie is lucky to have you as a mom."

"You really mean that?" she said, her eyes filling with tears again.

"I really mean that."

Melb sniffed and put away her tissue. "I guess I am lucky. I have an adorable son, and at my age, it's a miracle he's even here. I have great friends," she said, perking up, "and a terrific husband. You should see Oliver, Ainsley. He's so great as a dad. The other day, I asked him to change Ollie's diaper, and he had literal tears in his eyes. He just loves it so much."

"I know. Wolfe is so torn up about having to do this play. He said he feels like he needs to be more involved in the community for Abigail's sake. I can really respect that. He wants to keep Skary the way it is for his daughter."

"Huh," Melb said. "That's exactly what Oliver said."

"We have ourselves a couple of good men, and two beautiful babies to boot!" Ainsley stood. "You ready to keep walking?"

"Yeah, but let's head south. I don't want him to accidentally look at the sun and go blind."

Alfred, by his own admission, had actually become an expert on small town life. He'd never admit that publicly, and back in New York he cursed the slow pace of Skary and pretended to embrace the madness of the city.

But in a moment of honesty, there was something attractive about it all. For one, you had strolling, a lost art in the bigger cities. People here strolled in a way that made you think twice about honking at them at a crosswalk. Not that crosswalks were needed. If you closed your eyes and crossed the street in the middle of daylight, there was a ninety-eight percent chance you wouldn't get hit by a car…the same chance you had, however, of starting rumors about your own mental health, but that was another story.

The story at hand was *A Very Skary Christmas Carol.* Under his left arm, he carried a bundle of five hundred fliers, half red, half green. He'd driven thirty-seven miles just to find a copy shop. Skary had a pay-to-use copier, but Alfred could've typed out each flier faster than it copied, plus it had a fondness for putting a vertical line down the left side of the page.

These fliers were classy and straight to the point. There was going to be an *event* in Skary. Not a play. Not a gathering. An *event* that you were never likely to see again, so grab your chance now, while it was here. For a *short* time. There was nothing like creating a frenzy. In the publishing world, it was as easy as throwing out first print run numbers.

Or bringing Wolfe to a bookstore for a "rare" signing. And that part was true. Getting Wolfe to do signings back in the day was like pulling teeth. Alfred sighed. Back in the day. What a far cry he was from that. He'd gone from life with two secretaries and a corner office in a high-rise building to passing out fliers in…where was he again? This town didn't even have a sign. And it barely passed for a town. A couple of restaurants, a gas station, a street corner crowded with a few shops, and four empty warehouse buildings summed it up.

The key was the restaurant. Small-town folk liked to gather at restaurants. Diners, to be exact. It had taken a while, but Alfred had eventually gotten acclimated to their food source. He thought it really ironic. They lived among fields of ripe vegetables and fruit, yet it was remarkable how they could kill nearly every health benefit of any vegetable or fruit.

Corn, they creamed it. Okra, they fried it. Carrots, they buttered it. Sweet potatoes, they buried in brown sugar and topped with marshmallows. If it was a fruit, it ended up in a pie or a jam. Upon first arriving to Skary many years ago, he'd actually made a trip to the hospital one night after one of these meals, fearing a heart attack. Turned out it was, of all things, indigestion.

Alfred liked fish, himself. Preferably raw and wrapped in seaweed. He wasn't a vegetarian, but he didn't eat much meat, and most of the time just preferred salad. However, since his life had come to a screeching halt when Wolfe decided to go religious on him, Alfred had embraced the amazing phenomenon called *comfort food*, along with a spare tire around his waist. But he had never known mashed potatoes could be so good.

Crossing the only paved street in town, Alfred headed for the diner. The smell drifted ahead of him, drawing him in. A large sign boasted a thirty-two-ounce chicken-fried steak, and you got the next one free if you could eat the first one. Then you'd be dead, but at least you'd set a record, which it claimed had yet to be done.

Swinging the door open, the little bell rang as if you might not be noticed if it didn't announce you. An impossibility, really. You were always noticed when you walked into a small-town diner. Everyone looked up to see who had arrived. It had taken him some time to get used to that. In New York, nobody looked around, and nobody noticed who came and went from restaurants.

He drew a special amount of attention since he was not a regular patron of "these parts." Determined to make this work to his advantage, he focused on the lady with her hair in a net and whose Depends were apparently in a wad too.

"Help you?" she asked, her fist on her hip and her gum smacking itself to death.

"Alfred Tennison," Alfred said, careful to bring out his New York accent and his big city aura. He held out a hand for her to shake, knowing full well that she wouldn't do any such thing.

"So?"

"I've come to bring you good news."

"Really." She didn't say it, but he knew it. He could kiss her grits.

He pulled out a flier. "Skary is putting on a Christmas production."

The restaurant actually quieted. The lady, whose name tag read Betsy, glanced over the flier. "*A Very Skary Christmas Carol*? So what?"

"This is actually a *theatrical* production." Play sounded too run-of-the-mill. Production insinuated there might be a fog machine. Possibly pyrotechnics.

"What's it about?"

"Christmas. Skary-style." He liked that. Skary-style. Wasn't that the truth? Nothing happened anywhere quite like it did in Skary, Indiana.

"Well, this ain't Skary."

Oh, boy. His errand wasn't running very smoothly.

"This is going to be an unprecedented event. It's based on the book. It's called *A Christmas Carol.* It's actually a classi—"

"I don't care if it's called *A Christmas Betsy.* Don't interest me."

Alfred was losing patience. "Ever heard of Scrooge?"

She crossed her arms. "Yeah. He's standing here wasting my time." She grabbed her towel and went off to clean a table.

Alfred sighed. Maybe he should leave a stack of fliers by the door and move on. Or, better yet, put them on the windshields of the trucks outside. Of course, guys around here didn't like guys like

Alfred touching their trucks, and besides, the trucks were so huge that Alfred wasn't sure if he could even reach the windshields.

"You...yes, you..."

Alfred turned to find an older gentleman by himself in a nearby booth. He beckoned Alfred over with a crippled hand, frozen by arthritis. "Me?"

"How many 'yous' are there in here?" Was that a trick question? The old man smiled. "I know everybody by name in here. Except you." He stood with a great deal of effort and held out a hand for Alfred to shake.

"Alfred Tennison."

"Say again?"

"Alfred. Tennison," Alfred said, stressing each syllable.

"Obediah Graham." He sat back down and gestured for Alfred to sit with him. "You can call me Obie. And if you do call me, talk loud because I'm hard of hearing." Sliding into the booth, Alfred wondered what this man wanted. He looked kind enough. Maybe he just wanted some company. Alfred could relate. "What's that big stack of papers you got there?"

"Information on a huge Christmas production...event...that Skary is putting on this year."

"Oh, how nice." And it wasn't sarcastic, either. He looked genuinely pleased, but Alfred couldn't assume the man had actually heard what he'd said. Obie leaned toward him. "You know, Alfred, that's what we're missing these days. Something like what you're doing. Brings the whole community together to remember the reason for the season."

"Of course. What other reason would there be?"

"You're doing the Christmas story?"

Alfred chuckled. Obie was probably remembering Jean Shepherd, the wonderfully witty satirist who entertained an entire generation of radio listeners and penned the now-classic movie, *A Christmas Story.* And he supposed everyone in Indiana remembered Shepherd too, since the movie makes several references to the Indiana town of Hammond, where Shepherd grew up.

"I love Shepherd."

"I'm fond of the wise men."

"He was a wise man." Alfred was about to make reference to Shepherd's book *In God We Trust, All Others Pay Cash* when Obie pointed to the fliers.

"So what are you doing with those?"

"Oh, um, I'm going to pass them out."

"Come again?"

"Pass them out. To people. Let them know about the production."

"The what?"

"Play. The play." Alfred was talking loud enough for people to glance at him. Hey, it wasn't his fault Obie didn't like hearing aids.

"Ah, yes." His expression went skeptical. "You're not from around here, are you?"

"No."

Obie lowered his voice and Alfred had to wonder if he could even hear himself speak. "It's word of mouth around here, buddy boy. I know you big city people like to do it the fancy way, with green and red paper, special, elaborate type on the page." Skary was big city? That was scary.

"But the way to get things done around here is to…start spreading the news." Obie sang the last few words in perfect pitch, then chuckled to himself. Spry old guy. "I think our town needs to hear this message, Alfred. Christmas has become just another day of the year here. Puts people in a bad mood. Makes neighbors gripe at each other. Families can't stand to be with one another for more than half a day. And it seems to me, it's just another holiday where they can serve alcohol in the name of festivities." A sad expression crossed Obie's face. "They need to understand what it is to give a gift, and what gift has been given to us."

Alfred nodded, but the old man had gone nostalgic or something, so Alfred was having a hard time following the conversation, except for the parts about bad moods and alcohol.

Obie looked intently at the stack of fliers on the table. He sipped his tea, and with each sip, a growing determination emerged atop his weathered skin. "I'm going to help you." He set his cup down and lightly slapped the top of the table. "Yesiree. I'm going to help you."

"Help me do what?"

"Spread the good news, what else? We're going to start talking this thing up, Alfred. Ditch those silly things," he said, pitching his thumb toward the fliers. "We're going to start talking, and we're not going to stop until everyone hears about this." His eyes grew bright with memories. "Oh, I remember the time, Alfred. I remember it well. We'd do the play every year. It didn't matter, rain or snow. Sometimes we would even do it outside if we didn't have a good place to go. People would come from all over to see it. They'd tell their relatives, who would tell their relatives. Huge crowds!" Obie spread his arms wide. "I want to see that again, Alfred. I want a Christmas to remember."

"Indeed," Alfred smiled. "Indeed."

"So don't you worry about a thing. You hear me? You walkin' around here passing out fliers isn't gonna do a bit of good. People'll just be suspicious about you. We'll get people's mouths going, and nothing will stop it."

This would be an easy way to earn a buck. Alfred pulled out a business card from an inside pocket of his coat and handed it to Obie. "My cell phone number is on there. Call me if you need anything."

"Sonny, I have a phone, but I can't hear it ring. If you need to get ahold of me, call me up here. I eat breakfast, lunch, and dinner in this place, seven days a week."

Alfred withdrew his card. "Certainly." He stood, grabbing his stack of fliers. He still wasn't sure this was the best move. He hardly knew this guy. He could be senile or one to promise things he couldn't deliver. Alfred would use his help, but not rely on it. He couldn't take a chance with Obie and his trail of words.

Obie stuck out his hand. "Nice meetin' you."

"You, too, Obie. Thanks for your help." Alfred walked outside, the little bell announcing that he had left. It had turned colder now, and a brisk wind hit him, causing him to tuck his face into the collar of his coat. This was the creamed corn of all marketing plans, but maybe, just maybe, it would work.

CHAPTER 8

> "Mercy!" he said. "Dreadful apparition, why do you trouble me?"
>
> "Man of the worldly mind!" replied the Ghost, "do you believe in me or not?"

"FRED, FRED, FRED, Fred, Fred," Lois said, waving her arms.

"It's Dustin."

"I'm addressing you by your *character's* name. Because you're supposed to be in *character*. In other words, don't be you. Be the opposite of you. That's what I'm wanting, okay? Dustin, bye-bye. Hello Fred."

Dustin ran his fingers through his hair and let out a sigh. "I'm not sure I should be doing this, Lois—"

"Ms. Stepaphanolopolis to you, Dustin. When you hit thirty or can get a line out without saying 'like,' you can call me Lois."

"Ms. Stepa…Stephi…Sterpa—"

Lois sighed. "What's the question?"

"When you called me for this part, you didn't say anything about, like, being exciting."

"Fred is not exciting, Dustin. He's an optimist. Can't you see it in the text here? Scrooge is beating him down with his own words, yet Fred doesn't give up on his uncle. Don't slouch and stick your hands in your pockets, okay? Get that dirty hair out of your face and pretend to be a gentleman. Fred was a gentleman, okay?"

"Okay."

"But Scrooge is the victim here, got it? Oliver, from the top."

Dustin held up a finger. "But when Scrooge says I should be boiled in my own pudding and buried with a stake of holly through my heart, can I scream and writhe and can we have blood squirting out of my shirt?"

"Dustin, it's just rhetoric," Oliver said. "He's not actually going to—"

Lois interrupted. "Oh yes, he is, but none of that is going to matter if Fred isn't an optimist. Don't you see? Boiling pudding is symbolic for the death of optimism, and if Fred isn't optimistic, the entire idea is going to be lost on the audience, no matter how much blood we have squirting around."

Oliver sighed. "All this talk of pudding is making me hungry."

Lois thought for a moment and then turned to Dustin. "You need to draw inspiration from somewhere." She paused, rubbing her chin. "I know. I want you to call Ainsley Boone up and ask to follow her around for a full day."

"Why?"

"Because Ainsley is an optimist, Dustin. She's to Skary what Fred is to Scrooge. She always sees the good in everything. She's perky, polite, polished. Okay? Do you think you can do that?"

He shrugged. "I'm not sure about perky, but I'll give it shot."

"Good. Go on, now. Don't waste any more time. Marlee, come on up here."

Marlee, dressed in a suit that had "modern-day 1884" written all over it, stepped onto stage with three-inch spiked heels and a matching bodice. "Yes, Marlee! That's the look that I was hoping for! Excellent! It's a cross between Marie Antoinette and Ivanka Trump. Very good. I'm going to have to add some entrails, but you're on the right path." Lois paused. "Now, we're going to work on the scene with Cobb-Marley and Scrooge. Oliver, sit in that chair. Marlee, stand near the fireplace." The actors got into place. "Great. Now remember, Oliver, you're terrified of Jae Cobb-Marley. She was your business partner, and here she is, back from the grave."

Oliver gazed at Marlee. "Um…she doesn't look that terrifying. Is she a feminist?"

"Believe me, with some makeup adjustments, she's going to look frightful. And I'm toying with the idea of using that spiked heel in some wicked way. But for now, you're just going to have to use your imagination."

Oliver nodded, took in a deep breath, then gawked at Marlee like he'd seen a ghost. Perfect.

"Hear me!" Marlee recited. *"My time is nearly gone!"*

"I will," said Oliver, doing his best frightened imitation. *"But don't be hard upon me! Don't be flowery, Jacob…*I mean *Jae. Pray!"*

"How it is that I appear before you in a shape that you can see, I may not tell. I have sat invisible beside you many and many a day, in Versace no less."

"Now shiver!" Lois exclaimed. "Think quarterly tax payments."

Oliver wiggled his body.

"That is no light part of my penance," Marlee continued. *"I am here tonight to warn you that you have a chance and hope of escaping my fate. A chance and hope of my procuring, Ebenezer."*

"You were always a good friend to me."

"You will be haunted by three spirits."

"Is that the chance and hope you mentioned?"

"It is."

"I think I'd rather not."

"Without their visits, you cannot hope to shun the path I tread. Expect the first tomorrow, when the bell tolls one."

"Couldn't I take them all at once, and have it over, Jae?"

"Good Oliver, keep it up," Lois encouraged. "Imagine...you've just moved into a new tax bracket..."

"Expect the second on the next night at the same hour. The third upon the next night when the last stroke of twelve has ceased to vibrate. Look to see me no more; and look that, for your own sake, you remember what has passed between us!"

Lois ran onto stage. "Good! Good! Now, Marlee, you're going to back up slowly to the window. That's right, one step behind the other. Widen your eyes so you look like a zombie. Wider...still wider... Pretend you're the mayor at a town hall meeting... There you go. That's the look I want. Glue it to your face. Now, once you're at the window, beckon Scrooge... Uh, no, not with one finger like you're a floozy...your whole hand, slowly... Good. Now, Oliver, you're going to rise, and with great trepidation, walk toward her."

Lois watched the scene play out in front of her. The entire stage sustained silence except the light tap of Oliver's shoes as he crept toward Marlee, who did her best to look fearsome despite the chignon.

Finally, Oliver reached Marlee, and just when he was going to turn to ask, "What next?" Lois let out the most frightful scream ever heard from a human being. Which was followed by a scream from Marlee, who crashed backward into the window prop, tipping it over. Oliver shook like he'd just been electrocuted, but not a sound came from his wide-open mouth. He did, however, clutch his chest.

When Marlee stopped yelping and Oliver's color returned, Lois smiled. "Terrified?"

"What was that for?" Oliver demanded.

"I'm just giving you a taste of what the audience is going to go through during that scene. I want them to see it through Ebenezer's eyes, how terrifying it must've been for him."

"To see his old friend as a ghost predicting his doom?"

"Of course that. But we have to look deeper than the physical realm."

"I thought we were in the spiritual realm."

"Deeper."

Oliver and Marlee glanced at each other.

"Don't you see the conspiracy unfolding here? It's his old partner. Maybe returning for one more paycheck?"

"But why'd you have to scream like that?" Oliver asked.

"Because, Oliver, that's what happens in the book. Ebenezer goes over to the window, the ghost's hand lifts, and he hears horrifying and ghostly wailings. And I say, why just leave it at wailings? Why not kick it up a notch to bloodcurdling screams?"

Oliver wiped the sweat from his brow with a shaky hand. "Fine. But next time why don't you let us know ahead of time, okay?"

CHAPTER 9

"It is required of every man," the Ghost returned, "that the spirit within him should walk abroad among his fellowmen, and travel far and wide; and if that spirit goes not forth in life, it is condemned to do so after death. It is doomed to wander through the world—oh, woe is me!—and witness what it cannot share, but might have shared on earth, and turned to happiness!"

EARLY IN THE MORNING, Alfred drove toward… Where was he going again? Hobbieville. He reached for the map and wondered if gravel qualified for a road and whether or not it would be on a map. It amazed him how hard it was to find one thing out in the middle of nowhere. He came to a screeching halt, which is really impossible on gravel, and swerved, narrowly missing… What *was* that? Gripping the steering wheel, he tried to catch his breath. But suddenly a man jumped in front of his car. Holding a rifle. Alfred gasped, staring at the man's intense eyes and his "get out of the car" gesture. He didn't really want to, but the person with the gun usually gets their way.

Alfred slowly emerged, keeping his hands pointed toward the sky. "Don't shoot me," he said.

The man stepped forward, adjusting his John Deere hat and looking Alfred over. "What makes you think I'm going to shoot you?"

"The gun."

The man glanced at it like he hadn't realized it was there. "This ain't for you. It's for that deer you nearly ruined for me."

"Ruined?"

"I know what you're thinking: dead is dead. But road kill isn't edible." He looked off in the direction of where the deer ran. "Dang it. And the wife was going to make venison stew tonight."

"Oh...sorry," Alfred said, trying to sound equally disappointed about the venison stew. He didn't think he was pulling it off, though, so he changed the topic as he finally put his hands down. "I'm looking for Hobbieville."

The man chuckled. "Seems like you're not looking too hard now, are you?"

"Um...I've been following a map. There's supposed to be a road somewhere around here—"

"This is the road." The man pointed to the hill just up ahead. "About a half a mile, and you're there."

"Thanks. And...um..." Alfred gestured toward the gun. "Good luck with the venison." He got in his car and was about to pull forward when the man came up beside him and motioned for him to roll his window down.

"We're not quite finished here."

"Why?"

"You're a visitor."

"But not of the intergalactic variety," Alfred joked.

Venison Man didn't look amused. "Where are you from?"

Alfred wasn't sure New York was the best answer. "Skary."

"No kidding?"

"No kidding."

"I like Skary."

"Oh. Good. Me too."

"Planning on being there for that thing."

"What thing?"

"That big Christmas getup they're doing."

"The lights?"

"No, the production. The Christmas play."

"Really?"

"You're not going?"

"Uh...no, I am. I'm just... I was just coming to spread the news about the play." Alfred patted the fliers next to him. "How did you hear about it?"

"From Pete, Janet's uncle on her mom's side."

"Oh." Alfred glanced to the hill ahead. "Where can I get a cup of coffee?"

"At the gas station. Straight ahead."

"How about a bite to eat?"

"At the gas station. They got rest rooms too. Sign says Employees Only, but tell 'em Burt sent you, and they'll give you the key."

"Right."

"You go right, and you'll be plowing down a cornfield. Go straight, and you can't miss it."

Alfred rolled up his window, gave a short wave, customary in these parts, then went straight ahead. There, on the other side of the hill, was the gas station. Ironically, he didn't need any gas.

After he stopped the car, he opened the door, trying to hold it steady against the winter wind, and hurried inside, clutching his fliers. The attendant, standing behind the counter smoking, couldn't muster up an expression, but nevertheless felt free to stare.

"Howdy." No matter how many times Alfred tried that, it just didn't come out right, and always gave him away. "Got coffee brewing?"

The man pointed to his left. A large sign announced their new cappuccino maker, which wasn't a cappuccino at all but rather some concoction of sugar, chemicals, dairy product, and possibly coffee. The three flavors included pumpkin spice, chocolate-vanilla-caramel delight, or Irish Cream. Next to it was the regular coffee, which Alfred decided on. Thirty-two ounces of it.

Balancing the coffee and the fliers, he managed to throw down a couple of bucks at the counter. Just for kicks he asked, "Rest rooms?"

"Not open to the public."

"Burt sent me."

"Why didn't you say so?" The smoking attendant reached for the key. "Pull the door tight, or it'll pop open and embarrass the day-lights out of everyone standing on aisle four."

"Right. Listen, maybe I'll wait a minute and drink my coffee."

"Suit yourself." The man put the key away.

Alfred noticed a small crowd through the glass door that led to the diner. He walked toward it, trying to gather a game plan. He figured his best move would be to keep using Burt's name like a secret code.

As usual, the crowd looked up as he entered. There were people eating stacks of pancakes and others digging into french fries and burgers. Alfred steadied himself and waved. "Hey everyone. Wanted to give you some news."

The waitress, a younger woman and the friendliest face in the room asked, "Good news?"

"Skary is putting on a Christmas production. An event." Alfred withdrew one of the fliers and held it up. "And you're all invited."

"I heard something about that," the waitress said.

"Mo told us about that yesterday," someone said.

"Can't remember the last time we had something like that around here," said another.

Alfred smiled. He couldn't recall anything ever being this easy. He tucked away the flier in order not to jinx a rolling snowball's worth of good luck. "So you're all coming?" he asked.

The crowd nodded. The waitress said, "Why don't you come on in? We're still serving breakfast if you want something."

Alfred set the fliers down and climbed onto the stool at the counter. "Omelets?"

"No, sorry. Scrambled or fried."

"Scrambled. Any fresh fruit?"

"We have apple butter for your toast, or grape jelly if you prefer. You want sausage or bacon for your side?"

"Sausage, I guess."

"And I see you already got yourself some coffee," she said with a smile. "Next time just come on in. It's free over here."

"Thanks. I will."

She put the order in and came back to him. "I just called my grandparents and told them about the play. They're planning on coming. I hear it's going to be the most amazing thing we've ever seen!"

"Well...uh, I don't know if it's—"

"Are you going to have animals? Live animals?"

Alfred tried not to look as confused as he felt, and maybe it was because he was used to Broadway, but as far as he knew, there wasn't a petting zoo planned. However, whatever gimmick would bring people in, he was for it, though he couldn't really guarantee anything more than chickens and black cats. "You never know what's in store," he said and grinned.

"This is taking me back to my childhood," the waitress said, her eyes turning dreamy. "My grandparents used to always take us to this play. I loved it so much. I'm so glad to see it back. And this year, I'm going to vow to read the entire story to my kids on Christmas Eve."

Okay...well, good for her. If he could, in some small way, contribute to the advancement of literature, wasn't all this worth it? Especially without the help of fliers. The speed at which news flew from one place to another around here must set some sort of record. Small towns may have a slow pace, but they sure have some advanced way of spreading information—and fast. This could give dial-up a run for its money.

"There's even going to be a little bit of a twist to the story."

"Really?" Her face lit up again with excitement. "I didn't even realize there could be a twist."

"Well, every story has its interpretation, right? People come to it with their own worldview and take away from it things that are meaningful to them. This story has been told hundreds of times. For example, I'm sure everyone who has read it has a different picture in their mind of what the ghosts look like."

"You mean the angels?"

Alfred rested both arms on the counter. "See? You've proven my point. I say ghosts, you say angels."

She nodded thoughtfully. "I guess you're right. Never thought of it like that before." She held out her hand. "I'm Denise, by the way."

Alfred shook it gently. "Denise, it's a pleasure to meet you. I'm Alfred."

She laughed. "I know who you are! You almost killed Burt's deer for him!"

Ainsley rubbed Wolfe's shoulder as she cradled Abigail in the other arm. "Honey, I know you don't want to go, but you're doing Lois a huge favor. And the whole town is getting behind this production. People are already making plans to attend!"

Wolfe did look pathetically miserable.

"Abigail will be fine." She smiled. "She misses her daddy, but I tell her you'll always be back."

Wolfe let out a sigh as he stared at the front door. "I suppose if I must go…"

Ainsley watched his gaze hover at the door. She hated to see him like this. He'd stayed up half the night worrying about what Charles Dickens would think about it. Ainsley kept having to remind him that Dickens was dead.

Lacing her fingers between his, she said, "Wolfe, you know what?

Don't go. Don't do this. It's early enough. Lois can find someone else."

Wolfe's eyes widened with surprise. "Oh…no, I couldn't do that to Lois."

"There's plenty of time to find someone else. What about Martin?"

"No. The mayor's already playing Bob Cratchit." Wolfe waved his hands. "Look, I need to stop complaining. I'll go do it, do the best I can to salvage the play, and that will be that."

"Are you sure?"

Wolfe nodding emphatically as he grabbed his coat from the closet. "So I guess I better go study my lines. I'll pop in later, okay?"

"Uh…" But he was out the door. Ainsley held Abigail upright and nudged her nose against the baby's. "Your father! Always a writer!" She laughed. "Is that what you want to be when you grow up? A writer? Well, I suppose I could tolerate two writer-type personalities. Just promise me you won't die a thousand deaths at a bad review, okay?" She walked to the kitchen, laid Abigail in her playpen, and was about to do some dishes when a knock came at the door. Wiping her hands, she went to answer it.

"Hi," said Dustin, standing—well, slouching—there with a large smile. "It's Dustin. From the bookstore."

"Hi, Dustin," Ainsley said. "What brings you by?"

"Umm…like…can I come in?"

"Sure." Ainsley opened the door wider, and Dustin strolled in, glancing around the house.

"Huh."

"What's wrong?"

"I dunno. I just pictured Boo's house a little different, you know? I mean...it seems so normal." He shrugged. "I guess when you married him, things changed, right?"

"Not really. I've added a few touches, but Wolfe always had a nice decorating sense about him. His house was beautiful when I met him."

"That stinks," Dustin said. "I thought maybe he had trapdoors and stuff."

"So...what brings you by?"

"There used to be rumors he had a guillotine in the basement."

"No."

"What's that smell?" He looked at the counter and pointed. "That! What's that?"

"Puréed turkey."

Dustin covered his mouth and stepped a few feet away, uncovered his mouth, and seemed to breathe better. "Uh, yeah, anyway, I'm supposed to follow you around."

"Why?"

"Lois wants me to be more like you. My character, I mean. Fred."

"Not following."

"She says you're an optimist. My mom sees one of those for her contact lenses."

"Uh, Dustin, an optimist is someone who is positive."

"I know. I'm just making a play on words. It means overly positive."

"Not *overly.* Just positive."

"Okay..." Dustin already looked bored. "So can I hang around you today?"

Ainsley glanced at Abigail. "I'm pretty much just doing the mom thing, you know? I don't know how exciting that's going to be."

Dustin inspected his fingernails. "I guess that's what Lois means. Maybe she wants me to see what you're like around the baby versus what Wolfe's like."

"What Wolfe's like? What do you mean?"

"You know, how it drives him crazy and stuff."

Ainsley put her hands down on the counter, her fingers spread wide. "You're going to have to explain yourself."

Dustin's eyes lit up as he pointed into the kitchen. "Oooo! I love the hatchet!"

"That's a meat pounder. You were saying…?"

Dustin's eyes still roamed the room as he talked. "You know, just see what makes this so fun or whatever."

Ainsley's mind turned over the eighteen hundred possible interpretations of what Dustin had said, and he noticed the silence. "So, uh, this is what you do in the mornings? Put turkey in a blender?"

"Let's go back for a moment, Dustin," Ainsley said, trying to control each word that wanted to jump out. "You were talking about driving Wolfe crazy?"

"Not you. The whole baby thing."

"What whole baby thing?"

"You know, how he gags at the smell. He told Oliver he has nightmares about Abigail vomiting all over him."

"She's not vomiting. She's spitting up. Well, usually, except recently when she had that stomach thing…" Ainsley glanced at Dustin, who looked disgusted. "What else?"

"Nothing, dude. I mean, he's fine as long as he can go to play practice."

"What are you talking about?"

"So he doesn't have to change diapers." Dustin glanced at the turkey. "I don't blame him, if that's what she's eating." He actually looked pale.

"You're saying that he's doing this play just so he can get out of changing diapers?"

"No, not just the diapers. He also takes naps behind the stage. I have to tell you, the guy looks like he could invest in some eye drops."

"I can't believe this! He's pretending to be interested in doing this play just so he can get out of diaper duty? He's a little tired, so he thinks he can just go off and take a nap? I'm tired too! I'm in this house all day too! I'm the one who has to purée the turkey! And the spinach! And every other horrible smelling food that was never meant to be creamy! And to be such a coward about it! To leave under the guise of caring about a stupid play that he doesn't even want to be involved with in the first place!"

Ainsley's chest heaved in and out. She felt like she could burst into tears at any moment.

"So," Dustin said, leaning on the counter, "this is optimism, huh?"

CHAPTER 10

> "I am a mortal," Scrooge remonstrated, "and liable to fall."
>
> "Bear but a touch of my hand there," said the Spirit, laying it upon his heart, "and you shall be upheld in more than this!"

"COME ON OUT, honey," Lois called from in front of the stage. But he wouldn't come out. "Irwin, let's go. I need you out here." Lois sighed and looked at Oliver. "What is going on?"

Oliver stood there in a nightcap and nightgown he kept complaining was too short. "Maybe it's—"

"I look like an idiot!" came a reply from behind the curtains.

"Honey, come on, now. It's a play. This is your costume. It's not like you're going to be patrolling the streets in it."

"I will lose all respect. I will hear about this for months. There is no way I'm showing myself in this."

Lois crossed her arms. "I stayed up all night sewing that thing. You're telling me you're not going to wear it now?"

A few seconds passed, and then the sheriff peeked his head through the curtains. In one hand he clutched a branch of holly. In the other, a flashlight. "Come on," Lois urged in the tone she used when she meant there was really no need for the other person to decide what he wanted.

With a sigh and an eye roll, the sheriff came stomping out. The white tunic Lois had sewn looked perfect, as well as the shimmery gold belt she'd made of sequins. She'd hand stitched bright yellow flowers along the bottom, near the hem. His arms flung out, and his expression said, *Happy?*

Oliver's own expression didn't help matters. "Close your mouth, Ollie," Lois whispered, then met the sheriff halfway. "Why are you *holding* the flashlight?"

"I just don't think this is going to work."

"Sure it is. You've got that other elastic belt on underneath your tunic, don't you?"

"Yes."

"You just stick the light in there at the middle of your lower back. Make sure the light is pointing up, not down."

"Why does he have to stick a flashlight under his costume?" Oliver asked.

"Because he is supposed to be glowing. Light is supposed to be radiating from him."

"Can't I just smile a lot and use that whitening toothpaste you got me?"

"Okay, look, we can worry about the light later. Let's just get into the rehearsal."

"But what about the rest of me?" the sheriff asked, adjusting his white, long-flowing wig. "I look like a girl!"

"No," Lois said, "you look like a child. Which is how you're supposed to look. Well, like a freakish child, but we haven't even done makeup yet."

"I don't think makeup is going to be needed," Oliver said.

"All right, look, let's just get the rehearsal going, boys. Oliver, you're going to be sitting on the bed. Irwin, you'll stand next to the bed. Oliver, let's start here in the script."

Oliver gathered up his gown as he sat in the bed. *"Are you the spirit, sir, whose coming was foretold to me?"*

"I am."

"Irwin, voice higher, lighter. Remember, you look like a fairy. Act like a fairy. Irwin, fairies don't scowl."

"Who and what are you?" Oliver continued.

"I am the Ghost of Christmas Past," Irwin said, this time his voice a little higher.

"Long past?"

"No. Your past."

"That's where they always get you—your past," Lois inserted.

"Please, I beg you, put on your hat!" Oliver continued.

"What! Would you so soon put out, with worldly hands, the light I give?" Irwin held out his hat. *"Is it not enough that you are one of those whose passions made this cap and force me through whole trains of years to wear it low upon my brow!"* It was the line, but Lois got the feeling the sheriff might be addressing her.

Oliver continued. *"I'm sorry. I didn't realize I had 'bonneted' you. What business do you have here?"*

"Your welfare! Rise, and walk with me!"

Lois rushed over between them. "Welfare. Do you see what's happening here? I'm going to have to think about this, but there's a good chance, Irwin, I may have you clutching a welfare check."

The sheriff groaned. Walking across the stage and trailing behind Scrooge, he kept his hands behind him, asking if he was backlit.

"There, there," Melb said, reaching for tissue after tissue. "Ainsley, I'm not sure I've ever seen you this upset."

The poor girl hadn't stopped crying since she'd come through the door over thirty minutes ago. Melb had been frantic to try to find out what exactly was going on, which she still wasn't sure about. Not to mention Dustin over there, trying his best not to stare. But he was, and it was getting on Melb's nerves. "What are you looking at?" she demanded.

Dustin's hand slid off his face as he sat upright. "I'm just watching."

"Well, there's nothing to see here, okay, buddy? So why don't you get out? I can take it from here."

Ainsley blotted her face. "No, it's okay, Melb. He can stay. He was kind enough to bring me over."

"Why is he bringing you over?"

Ainsley gave a sweet but sad smile in Dustin's direction. "He's basing a character on me."

Melb raised an eyebrow. "Interesting."

"It is," Dustin said. "I'd never thought of playing Fred this way, but it might work."

"He's supposed to be"—Ainsley burst into tears again—"an optimist."

"Yeah, sure, but maybe he's got some baggage, you know?" Dustin said. "I mean, that's what makes great characters. They're complex."

"There is nothing complex about this!" Ainsley exclaimed. "My husband doesn't want to be home with me!"

"What?" Melb gasped. "What in the world makes you think that?"

"I don't have to think it. Dustin told me so."

Dustin sank into his chair. "I didn't exactly say that."

"It's not his fault," Ainsley said, managing to get her crying under control. "He just let it slip...that Wolfe joined the play just so he could get out of the house."

Melb moved closer to Ainsley and took her hand. "I can't believe it's true."

"Dustin said he hates changing diapers and is exhausted and just wanted an excuse to get out of the house."

Dustin's face grew strained. "Look, I think you're, like, overanalyzing what I said."

"Oh? Now I'm overanalyzing too? No wonder he can't stand to come around me!"

"Calm down, Ainsley. There's got to be a reasonable explanation for this."

"Yeah, I mean, he loves you. And your kid too. He's always talking about you guys," Dustin said with a hopeful look, his eyes darting back and forth between Ainsley and Melb.

"You're just saying that to make me feel better."

"Honey," Melb said, "I think Dustin's right. You know how much Wolfe loves you."

"I thought I did. But maybe that was before I had this baby, put on some weight, and now look like some freaky monster from one of his books." She combed her fingers self-consciously through her disheveled hair.

"The vampire chick he had in three of his books was hot." Dustin's smile was short-lived.

Melb addressed Ainsley. "You're tired. He understands that. He's tired too."

"Yeah, too tired to come home and spend time with his family."

"He's not gone every night of the week."

"Unfortunately for him." Ainsley blew her nose and watched Abigail gurgle, lying on a blanket in the middle of the living room. Melb had put earmuffs on the baby so she wouldn't hear Ainsley crying.

Rubbing the middle of Ainsley's back, Melb said, "Ainsley, listen to me. This is a tough time. Believe me, I know. I've been through it. You're tired, your hormones are out of whack, and things can get blown out of proportion. You're seeing this as Wolfe not wanting to be around you, but in reality, I think it's just that Wolfe needs a little bit of time to himself. He's adjusting to being a dad. It's normal. Men just aren't wired like we are. None of this means that he doesn't love you and Abigail."

Uncertainty lingered in Ainsley's eyes.

"You should listen to her," Dustin said from across the room where he'd managed to relocate. "She knows what she's talking about."

Melb rolled her eyes. He was just trying to help, but Melb wished he would go away. She was about to suggest he do that very thing when he added, "Like Oliver, right?"

"What about Oliver?"

"I mean, that's where Wolfe got the idea, right?"

"What idea?"

"To do the play to get some time away from the house." The carefree expression slid off Dustin's face. "What?"

"Are you trying to tell me all of this was Oliver's idea?" Melb said. Well, roared.

Dustin actually looked like he might bolt for the door, but Melb stood up, so he sat down. "You're making this up."

"I swear, I'm not," Dustin said. "I heard them talking about it."

"Oliver would never do that! He loves little Ollie. Wants to spend all of his extra time with him. Every second of every day."

Dustin stuttered, gestured, and gulped. "But what about everything you were telling Ainsley here? About love and hormones and stuff?"

Melb stepped closer. "Let me tell you something, kid. And this is a lesson you'll want to take with you for the rest of your life. A man shall not, under any circumstance, ever utter the word 'hormone' in front of a woman."

He nodded with wide eyes.

"Now get out of here and leave us alone."

He hurried toward the door and flew down the porch steps. Melb returned to Ainsley, who was back to crying again. She sat next to her on the couch and took Ainsley's hands into hers.

With tears dripping down her face, Ainsley said, "It's going to be okay, right?"

Melb's nostrils flared. "It will be when we're done with them."

CHAPTER 11

It is always the person not in the predicament
who knows what ought to have been done in
it, and would unquestionably have done it too.

WOLFE SHRUGGED OFF his coat as he walked in the front door. Hanging it in the closet, he could hear sounds coming from the kitchen, and the smell beckoned him. Was it baked chicken? Mashed potatoes? He could hardly wait. He was starving.

"There's my girl!" Wolfe said as he walked up to the bassinet that held Abigail. She watched a mobile go round and round, but upon seeing Wolfe, her mouth opened wide as she tried to smile. He took her hand, and she grasped one of his fingers with all her might. He gently ran his thumb across the soft skin of her arm. "I'll be back. I'm going to go say hi to your mommy."

Strolling into the kitchen, he found Ainsley at the stove, stirring something in a pan. He prayed it was gravy. He loved her gravy. Coming from behind, he reached out and wrapped his arms around her.

She screamed.

Then she stumbled backward and knocked her elbow against the handle of the pan. It tipped up and scooted off the stove, crashing to the floor just as they both jumped out of the way. Gravy splattered across the cabinets like an impressionist painting. Ainsley stood glaring at it, then him.

"Honey, are you okay?" Wolfe rushed to her. "I'm so sorry. I didn't mean to scare you. I thought you heard me come in."

She held the wooden spoon like she was about to use it. On him.

"Um…here, let me help you clean this up." He rushed to the laundry room where he grabbed three rags. When he returned to the kitchen, Ainsley still hadn't moved. "Are you okay?"

"Why wouldn't I be okay?" She held out her arms as if on display. "The entire dinner is ruined now."

"No, no, honey. It's not ruined. It's just the gravy. You make the best chicken. It's always moist. There's no need for gravy." He stooped, started wiping, and looked up at her. "I'm really sorry."

She took a rag and dabbed at her pants. Wolfe wasn't sure, but she seemed disproportionately mad. Usually things like this made her just throw up her arms and laugh. He finished wiping the floor while Ainsley went over to check on Abigail. He put the rags in the laundry room and came out to find Ainsley back at the stove.

"Did you have a bad day?" he asked, rubbing her shoulders.

She stiffened and moved away from him. "Fine. Mind setting the table? Dishes are set out."

"I don't mind at all, but first I want to make sure you're okay."

The doorbell suddenly rang, and Wolfe could feel his stomach turn. He was early.

"Who is that?" Ainsley asked.

"Uh…Alfred."

"Why is he here?"

"I kind of invited him to dinner."

"What? Why would you do that?"

"Why would I do that? You're always telling me to invite Alfred for dinner. He's lonely, he doesn't have any friends, et cetera."

"It would've been nice for me to know. I don't know if I have enough food, especially with the gravy gone. I wasn't even sure you would be here tonight."

"Why wouldn't I be home for dinner?"

"I don't know. Maybe you needed more time to work on the play?"

The doorbell rang again.

"Well, don't just stand there and leave Alfred out in the cold."

Wolfe hustled to the door. Opening it, he greeted Alfred, who strolled in with…was that *glee* in his eyes? "Wolfe," he said, dropping his coat into Wolfe's hands, "sometimes I'm amazed at how smart I am." His nose lifted. "Ah. Chicken. That's one thing I love about your wife. She always knows just what to cook when I'm coming for dinner."

"I was just setting the table."

Wolfe trailed Alfred into the dining room, and then realized there were only two plates and two sets of silverware. "Have a seat. I'll be right back."

While Alfred made himself at home, Wolfe hurried to the kitchen. Ainsley still looked in a mood, but at least in front of Alfred she kept it subdued. "Honey," Wolfe said in a low voice, "I'm sorry if I've upset you. I am so sorry I spilled the gravy."

"It's fine," she mumbled. "Go set the table. I'll bring the food in after I change Abigail's diaper."

"Here, let me do that."

"No, don't worry about it." She walked past him and then took

Abigail upstairs. Sighing, Wolfe tried to gather a little composure before returning to Alfred who, most likely, would take and need all his attention.

Alfred had already helped himself to some wine and sat at the head of the table. He watched Wolfe set the dishes out. "You are quite domesticated, aren't you?"

"What does that mean?"

"Well, here you are setting the table, and not a word out of you. It's nice. Really. And you seem to be taking to fatherhood?"

"Alfred, I'm not going to waste any time trying to explain it all, but yes, it's the most wonderful thing you could imagine. Well, not *you,* but most people."

Alfred grinned. "So I'm a little self-centered. If it weren't for self-centered people, we wouldn't have stories like *A Christmas Carol* now, would we?"

Wolfe looked up. "You're doing the play?"

"No, I'm not 'doing' the play. I'm turning the play into an event. The buzz is incredible!"

"Buzz?"

"So far, I've got nearly every county within an hour of here ready to come and see the show." He held up his glass in a pretend toast. "If you can market something to people spread out by way of cornfield, you can market just about anything."

"How are you doing that?"

"The old-fashioned way, Wolfe. Door-to-door. Like the politicians used to do. You get one person behind it, and the next thing you know, the kin are in, and when the kin are in, you've struck gold."

Wolfe groaned. "Great. You're saying a lot of people are coming?"

"A lot is an understatement."

"Alfred, it's going to be horrible! I'm serious. It's going to be the worst thing you've ever seen."

Alfred crossed his legs, unconcerned. "Not my problem. My job is to get them in the door, and that's what I'm doing."

Ainsley appeared, carrying a platter of chicken and, thankfully, wearing a brighter expression. "Good evening, Alfred. I'm so glad you could join us." She set the chicken right in front of him. "Your favorite."

"Ainsley, my dear, you are the reason I return to this little town. Nobody cooks like you do."

Ainsley smiled graciously and returned to the kitchen for the rest of the food. Wolfe leaned in close to Alfred. "Alfred, listen, just do me a favor and don't rattle her cage tonight, okay?"

"Rattle her cage?"

"You know, talking about small towns and all that. Ainsley can usually take stuff like that, but she's not really in a good place right now."

Alfred raised an eyebrow. "Trouble at home?"

"No. It's just exhaustion, okay? Babies are a lot of work. Just be on good behavior. Is that too much to ask?"

Alfred served himself two pieces of the chicken Ainsley had already sliced. "Wolfe, you know I always mind my manners, at least around your wife." Alfred glanced up and took in Wolfe's worried expression. His fork and knife paused. "Good grief, don't have a nervous breakdown. I got the message."

Ainsley returned with a bowl of green beans in one hand and a bowl of mashed potatoes in the other. She avoided Wolfe's eyes but still kept up the pretense. Wolfe sighed, wishing he knew what was wrong.

Wolfe blessed the food Alfred had already begun eating, and the conversation hummed around what was going on with Alfred back in New York: pretty much nothing, but he had a talent for sounding like he was conquering the world.

Alfred made a moaning noise as he pointed to the chicken. "Ainsley, darling, this is fabulous. And I tell you, my life would be complete if I could have some of your famous gravy."

"No! No! Stage right! And would somebody ask Cyclops to cover his third eye?" Lois blinked, realizing she was waving her arms and shouting loudly, but she wasn't quite sure why. Or where she was. Or why Melb Stepaphanolopolis stood over her with an unhappy look on her face.

"Cyclops?" Melb asked.

"Did I say Cyclops?"

Lois glanced around, noticing the curtain. She'd been up the night before, reworking the scene with the Ghost of Christmas Yet To Come. She couldn't quite get him where she wanted him. Her eyelids still felt heavy as she looked blankly at Melb's scowl.

"I need to have a word with Oliver," Melb said.

"Oh, sure." Lois stood and peeked through the curtains. "I'll just get him—what in the name of Dickens are you two doing?" Lois shouted as she flung the curtains open and marched onto the stage. Oliver slumped in a chair while Garth messed with his costume. "Garth, stop it!"

Garth whirled around to face her, his arms flung wide open. "This is ridiculous! Do you know how bad I smell?" He gestured toward Oliver. "Look at him. He's about to pass out."

"It's not that bad," Oliver said. "But it does make me feel like I need to sauté you with a little olive oil and pour you into some marinara."

"Look," Garth said, "I went to the bookstore and bought this Dickens book. And, well, okay, the CliffsNotes, too. All right, only the CliffsNotes. But the point is that the book states that the Ghost of Christmas Present should be wearing some sort of furry green robe with a holly wreath set on top of his head. And a few icicles or something. Look at me!" He pointed to himself.

But in all actuality, nobody had to look at him. Everyone could smell him. That's because, in the name of continuity and tone, Lois had taken creative license and replaced the holly with garlic. It only made sense. He was a phantom, a specter, a ghoul…not a wreath! Holly and icicles? Please! That belonged on garland, not on her ghost.

"Aren't I the party ghost? Don't I bring Scrooge around to all the festivities? If I read the notes right, it seems like even Scrooge himself gets lost in the fun, forgetting that he can't even be heard or seen! And I'm supposed to be pointing out poor Tiny Tim, right? Who is going to listen to a guy with garlic wrapped around his head?"

"You must trust your director," Lois said calmly. "There is a lot of symbolism built into the garlic."

"I read the entire essay on symbolism! There is nothing about garlic in there!"

"No, but what many fail to see is the relationship between the ghosts."

"What do you mean?" Oliver asked.

"The Ghost of Christmas Yet To Come is by far the scariest ghost of them all. He is so frightening that even the Ghost of Christmas Present is terrified of him, which is why he wears the garlic."

A chirping cricket seemed to be the only thing with a pulse at the moment. Lois slapped her hands together. "Now, let's get on with it. Why weren't you running the scene I asked you to run?"

Oliver sighed. "Lois, we did. For forty-five minutes. But you disappeared."

Lois cleared her throat. "Well, I was in a creative trance. It happens sometimes. But now I am revived, so let's get on with it. Where are the puppets?"

Katelyn popped out, holding one sock with brown string hair—a boy—and the other sock with yellow string hair—a girl. Red-markered smiles and googly, stick-on eyes made up their expressions. She'd glued gummy worms all over each of them.

"Hello!" Katelyn said, pretending to be one of the puppets. She grinned proudly at Lois. "Aren't these great? I came up with the gummy worm thing to make them appear scary, like you asked. Aren't they adorable?"

"Adorable. Yes, that's what I'm going for, Katelyn. This entire piece is going to make everyone clutch their hearts and click their heels." Lois stomped forward. "Didn't you read my notes? They are supposed to be hideous!"

Katelyn's arms fell to her side. "They are. They've got worms coming out of their skin."

"Gummy worms. That's not going to scare anybody, Katelyn. I want people to feel faint, like they might lose their lunch. Do you hear what I'm saying? Nobody is going to buy into the idea that those two *puppets* are scary!"

Katelyn's bottom lip protruded. "I'm sorry. I don't know what else to do, but I'll give it another shot."

"Fine. But for now, we're just going to have to roll with it. This is a key scene, people, and I want it done right! Put everything you've got into it. Oliver, do you hear me? I want to see Scrooge dejected, frightened, humiliated, and humbled. Scared out of his mind. But still a little bit stubborn as he contemplates cheating on his taxes. All right? What am I going to have to do to pull this character out of you?"

"I'm trying, Lois. I really am. By the time we open, I'll have him."

Lois spun her finger in the air. "Fine. From the top of the scene. Let's go."

Everyone moved into place as Lois approached Melb, who still waited in the wings. "I'm sorry, Melb. Now is not a good time. Can't you just talk to Oliver when he gets home tonight?"

One eyebrow lifted high on Melb's forehead as she studied Oliver. "You say he's not getting the character?"

"Not really," Lois sighed. "He's trying. I'll give him that. But Scrooge needs to be in a perpetual state of moodiness. Do you know what I mean? He's got to be the guy that hates life and anyone who dares to live it. He's got to be miserable."

"I think I might be able to help you out with that."

"Oh?"

"Yes."

"Well, good. I need something. I have puppets that look like they belong on Sesame Street." Lois signaled for them to start.

Oliver began. *"Forgive me if I am not justified in what I ask, but I see something strange, and not belonging to yourself, protruding from your skirts. Is it a foot or a claw?"* he asked the ghost.

"It might be a claw," answered Garth, batting at the garlic swinging from his forehead, *"for the flesh there is upon it. Look here."* Garth parted his robe. Katelyn hunkered behind him and slid the puppets around the outside of each leg.

Oliver pretended to gasp in fright. He was supposed to look appalled, but it came off as annoyed. What would it take to make this man look *desperate*? *"Spirit, are…are they yours?"*

"They are Man's. And they cling to me, appealing from their fathers. This boy is Ignorance. This girl is Want. Beware them both and all of their degree, but most of all beware this boy, for on his brow I see that written which is Doom, unless the writing be erased!"

Suddenly, from the back of the auditorium, they all heard a scream. Lois stepped onto the stage and saw a shadowy figure standing near the back, who looked like he might faint. "Alfred?"

Melb stepped up beside her. "The puppets might be scarier than we think."

CHAPTER 12

> Somehow he gets thoughtful, sitting by himself so much, and thinks the strangest things you ever heard. He told me, coming home, that he hoped the people saw him in the church, because he was a cripple, and it might be pleasant to them to remember upon Christmas Day, who made lame beggars walk, and blind men see.

AFTER CONVINCING EVERYONE he was fine and just had the stomach flu, Alfred managed to escape the theater and all the people who had surefire ways to beat a virus. Suggestions ranged from standing in front of his open freezer for five minutes to grinding up tree bark and mixing it into milk.

He should've known the stomach flu line wouldn't work. In New York, all you needed to make people scram was the mention of a contagious disease. But in the backward way of Skary, Indiana, it actually caused people to line up on your doorstep to bring you chicken soup and washcloths for your forehead.

He'd come to the theater to tell Lois that he wouldn't need any more fliers. The news was spreading quickly and had even landed in some local newspapers. But just hearing those familiar words, although they were talking about sock puppets no less, caused fear to strike yet again, deep inside him. There had hardly been time to revel in his marketing accomplishment before being struck by that stupid little demon named Ignorance.

It haunted him as if he were Scrooge himself. And maybe he was. Maybe he was the Skary equivalent. The black trench coat in a room full of sundresses. The one dark bulb in a glowing white light strand. The guy that sings off-key in a church chorus. No, worse. He's the guy that can't even read the music.

That was him. Yes. He was looking at the same sheet music as everyone else, but he couldn't read it. He couldn't make sense of the notes. Or even the words, for that matter. He did a decent job keeping up appearances, but soon enough, everyone would know he was just lip-syncing.

The frigid air didn't keep him from plopping down on one of the many park benches that lined Main Street. He didn't want to go home. There was a good chance a company of carolers would happen by, and he would, no doubt, have to stand there and listen to it all with a cheery disposition.

"Hello, Alfred." Mayor Martin Blarty stood clutching his briefcase, earmuffs doing a good job of helping the cliché of this town along. Not to mention the Frosty the Snowman scarf wound around his neck.

"Hello, Martin."

"Are you looking for something?"

"Looking for something? I'm just sitting here."

"You look like you're looking for something."

Alfred could only shrug.

"Something bothering you?" the mayor asked.

Alfred pinched the bridge of his nose, then dropped his face into his hands. Well, why not? Why not blab about it all? What did he have to lose? It was eating him up inside, not to mention doing a poor job of hiding itself, evident in the fact that he'd been caught very much off guard, in the most humiliating way, at the theater just moments before.

Alfred shook his head and peeked at the mayor from behind his hands. "It's embarrassing, to tell you the truth, Martin."

The mayor smiled. "I've had my share of embarrassment. I'm sure I'll understand."

"I don't know. It's hard to explain."

"Give it a try."

"Okay. Well, it all started in my childhood. With Want."

The mayor smiled knowingly and sat down next to him on the bench. "Oh, sure. It happens to the best of us. Everybody wants more and more, right?"

"You don't understand. I was Ignorance."

"Not to give you a complex, but I think you mean you were *ignorant.*"

"I'm talking about the girl, Want, in the pl—"

"Been there. For a while, all I wanted was Lois Stepaphanolopolis. I gotta tell you, after seeing her direct this show, I can't help but think I'm pretty lucky not to have gotten what I wanted, if you know what I mean."

Alfred would have to take a different approach. How could he explain a phobia of two puppets? "That's the problem. I don't know what I want. I need something. I know that. I want to find it. But I don't know what it is. And if I did know, I wouldn't know how to get it." Alfred paused. "The very definition of ignorance. Maybe I've become the very thing I fear."

"Don't fear, Alfred. The Lord has a way of showing us not what we want, but what we need. Maybe you want for nothing. But maybe you need something."

"Need." Alfred pondered it. "Too bad that's not a character."

"What?"

"Nothing."

The mayor patted him lightly on the shoulder. "If it makes you feel any better," the mayor said with a sudden enthusiasm in his voice, "you must know, the phones are ringing off the hook."

"Phones? What phones?"

"Oh, all right. *Phone.* But it's been ringing like crazy. I finally had to hook up our old answering machine just to get out of the office tonight."

"About what?"

"About what? The play! I tell you, Alfred, I haven't seen this kind of excitement since we had that five-county parade seven years ago. People are really getting behind this thing." Martin grinned. "I'm playing Bob Cratchit. Did you know that?"

"No. I haven't hung around a lot... You know, been busy marketing."

"Well, you have quite a talent. It's remarkable. I've had people calling me to see if we're taking up an offering. Others have called wondering if we're going to allow flash photography. I even heard from one man offering to let us use his donkey!"

"His donkey? Why?"

Martin laughed. "I have no idea. But it's just that season. People become generous. Maybe that's all the guy has, you know? A donkey. But he was willing to haul it up here if we needed it. That's why I love this time of year. It brings out the best in everyone."

"Except Scrooge," Alfred pointed out wryly.

"Yes," Martin chuckled. "That Scrooge. Dickens had quite an imagination. Though I suppose every town has their own Scrooge. We had one. She died a few years back. Missy Peeple."

Who could forget that crazy old busybody? But Alfred nodded only vaguely.

"I thought we'd plan for hot chocolate and cookies after the show. Maybe you would like to do a reading, Alfred?"

"A reading?"

"Yes. Of *A Christmas Carol.* After the show. That would be perfect!" Martin said, slapping his mittened hands together. "That's something they do in New York, right? They have people stand up and read something."

Alfred stared at the empty street as the wind chilled his cheeks and caused him to quiver. "I'll have to think about it."

"And listen, Alfred, maybe you'll be flying back to New York for Christmas, but if not, I'd like to invite you to come for dinner. I'm having a few people over. Nothing extravagant, but we have fun. We usually get a game of Scrabble going, and we drink eggnog like it's really got alcohol." He laughed. "Oh, and bring a white elephant gift. That's the highlight of the evening." He leaned in. "And don't forget the Christmas Eve service. It's really something special. We sing 'Silent Night,' and everyone holds their candles in the air. That's my favorite part, except the year when Mr. Stone accidentally caught Mrs. Humphrey's hair on fire, but luckily it was just a wig, so everything turned out fine." Martin closed his eyes. "There's nothing like that song, you know? 'Silent night. Holy night. All is calm. All is—' "

"And don't you think for one second that I'm going to believe any of that nonsense!"

Alfred and Martin jumped to their feet and turned toward the commotion. A woman was shouting, and through the darkness, they could see her beating some poor guy over the head with her purse. "You are despicable!"

"It's Oliver! And Melb!" Martin said and began running toward them. Alfred decided to follow, although he figured that when the woman is beating up the man, there's no real need to get involved.

"You're being ridiculous!" Oliver said as he blocked purse shots.

"What's going on here?" Martin asked.

Melb, holding a small suitcase in her other hand, flung it at Oliver. "Don't even think about coming home tonight!" And with that, she stomped away.

The three men stood there, each staring at the suitcase that had hit Oliver in the chest and now lay at his feet.

"What's going on?" Martin whispered.

"I'm not sure. One minute, I'm running a scene; the next minute, I'm a lazy excuse for a husband." Oliver rubbed the top of his head. "I've never seen Melb this angry."

"What are you going to do?"

Oliver thought for a moment. "She mentioned something about Wolfe and Ainsley. I didn't catch all of it because she kept slapping my ears, but maybe they know something I don't." Oliver slowly crouched to lift the suitcase off the ground. "Well," he said, standing and adjusting his coat to sit straight across his shoulders, "you two gentlemen have a nice evening. Happy holidays."

Alfred shook his head. Now that was the kind of dysfunction that could get him in the holiday spirit.

CHAPTER 13

His offences carry their own punishment,
and I have nothing to say against him.

OLIVER TROMPED UP the long sidewalk that led to Wolfe and Ainsley's home. He checked his watch. There was a chance that Abigail was already in bed, so he would have to knock softly. The windows glowed with light, indicating someone was still up.

But before he could knock, the front door flew open. Ainsley stood there bundled up like she was ready for a hike. Abigail was wrapped in three blankets.

"Oliver?"

"Ainsley? Are you going somewhere?" Then he noticed the suitcase at her side. "You are?"

Tears welled up in her eyes. "I'm going to stay with Melb."

"Why?"

She glanced behind her. "Why don't you ask Wolfe?"

"He knows something? Because I'm confused. Melb yelled at me and threw me out of the house."

The tears dripped down her cheeks. "I don't think Wolfe will even notice I'm gone. All he wants is some peace and quiet." Her sorrowful eyes suddenly turned angry. She moved past him and walked to the side of the house where her van was parked.

Oliver stood in the doorway of the Boone home, uncertain what to do. Was Wolfe really here? Surely not, or he would've been clamoring out the door after her. And how could Ainsley and Melb both be mad at the same time? A sinking feeling came over him when Wolfe suddenly appeared out of his study, carrying a script with a pencil tucked behind his ear. He glanced up, and surprise popped onto his face. "Oliver?"

"Yes?" Oliver squeaked.

"What are you doing?"

"Just, uh…just standing here."

Wolfe came over. "Why?"

Oliver shrugged, having a hard time coming up with something to say. His suitcase started doing the talking as Wolfe's attention fell to it. "Um…well, Melb kicked me out."

"What? Why?"

"That's what I came over to find out."

Wolfe guided him in by the shoulders and shut the front door. "Sit here," he said, and Oliver slid onto a barstool. "You want tea?"

"Okay."

"Did you two have a fight?"

"Not that I'm aware of. I was at play practice, and she showed up. She started yelling at me about how I didn't want to be around her and that if they were that much trouble, she didn't want me around. Or something like that."

"And you can't think of anything you did to make her mad?"

"Nothing. I left for play practice, and she was fine. She even said she'd have some warm cider waiting for me when I got home."

Wolfe put the kettle on the stove. "Maybe Ainsley knows what's wrong. She was with Melb today. But between you and me," Wolfe whispered, "she's been acting a little strange too. I haven't had a chance to put up the Christmas lights, but she's throwing words out like 'obligation' and 'responsibility.' It's a strand of Christmas lights, you know? Anyway, let me just run upstairs, see if she's up to talking."

"Oh, um..."

"She might already be asleep. I haven't seen her since we finished dinner. I helped her clean the kitchen, and I've been working on my lines...well, my character anyway. I don't have any lines, but Oliver, I think I've nailed it. I really do. I've been practicing some mannerisms that I think are dead-on—"

Oliver stopped Wolfe as he passed by. "Wolfe, she's gone."

"What do you mean she's gone?"

"I saw her walk out. With a suitcase. And your daughter. They're staying at my house."

"That's absurd."

"It just happened. I was about to knock on your door, and there she was. She seemed upset."

Wolfe looked mortified.

Oliver continued trying to sort through everything. "What's going on? I mean, Melb, yeah, she's temperamental. But for Ainsley to be mad too...there's got to be something wrong. That can't be a coincidence."

"Hold on." Wolfe ran upstairs and within a few seconds came bounding back down with a piece of paper in his hand. "I knew it. She left a note."

"How did you know she would leave a note?"

"That's just Ainsley. She's very organized, even when she's angry." Wolfe tore open the envelope and pulled out a lined piece of paper.

"Well, what's it say?"

"Dear Wolfe, hope the play goes well. As for me and Abigail, we'll get out of your way so you can concentrate on doing what you love the most. We wouldn't want to be a burden. Ainsley."

Wolfe dropped the note to the counter. "What does this mean? She's mad because I'm doing the play and can't hang the Christmas lights?"

"Melb too?"

"I can't believe this! I've done nothing but comply with every whim and need of this family. I get up twice in the middle of the night. I change dirty diapers. I disinfect anything within a two-foot radius of Abigail. And this is what I get? She's mad because of some stupid Christmas lights? Well, you know what? She can be mad! At least now maybe I can get some sleep!"

Wolfe stormed up the steps, and Oliver heard the door slam. Goose's and Bunny's ears went up as they studied Oliver. The teakettle whistled, startling him to his feet. He took it off the burner, sighed, and opened the refrigerator. If all else fails, pillage the fridge.

Swollen, puffy, dark blue bags hung under Alfred Tennison's bloodshot eyes. Strangely, though he hadn't had a drop of alcohol, he felt hungover. His dreams wrestled his mind all throughout the night, until the morning sun demanded he rise. He couldn't be completely sure, and he wouldn't mention a word of it to anybody, but if he had to describe it, it was as if he were being...haunted. Not by ghosts, per se, though that might be preferable. Instead, it was by fear. His past, which he wished he could do away with, seemed chained to him. He was helpless. And desperate. This was the magic formula to get him back into the office of Jack Hass.

Dr. Hass twiddled his thumbs, lost in his own thoughts, gazing toward the ceiling. Alfred had explained it the best way he knew how, even throwing reputation to the wind as he described the sheer terror that had come over him when he heard those awful words from the stage.

It made him sound pretty kooky when he had to admit that the terror came from two sock puppets, but Dr. Hass, of all people, seemed to understand it was not so much the puppets as what they represented.

Finally, Dr. Hass leaned forward. "Alfred, I don't normally tell people to do this because frankly, not too many people really want to face their fears. But you have carried this for a long time, and I believe you're ready to be done with it once and for all."

Alfred fingered his jaw as he listened. He could barely nod, but he did.

"You must go and confront Ignorance and Want, face to face."

"Did I mention their eyes are glued on and they have marker smiles?"

"They're symbolic. Your mind is playing tricks on you, but the real issue is your past. And I think we need to bring Tiny Tim into this conversation."

"Why?"

"Because at the root of all this is the fact that Tiny Tim hurt you. And the irony, I suppose, is that he is a gentle-natured boy."

"Leave it to me to embody irony."

"So you're going to go confront your fears. You will find these puppets, and Tiny Tim, and you're going to stand there and tell them that your life is yours and not theirs, that they may no longer steal your joy."

"Uh..."

"No. Alfred, if you want to get better, you are going to have to do this. There's no hesitation. No second thoughts. You go and do it now."

Alfred slumped in his seat. The irony continued as he realized the puppets and Tiny Tim could both be found in the same place—Katelyn Downey's home. She made the puppets, and her son, Willem, played the part of Tiny Tim. Fighting his demons turned out to be convenient. That couldn't be overlooked.

Alfred managed to stop fiddling with anything within reach and said, "All right, I'll go."

Melb and Ainsley sat at Melb's breakfast bar. The babies were content on the floor, indulging in the flashing lights and electronic music of their baby toys. But the two women were not content. Ainsley watched Melb pick up the receiver of the phone one more time, hold it to her ear, and then set it back down. "It's working. I hear a dial tone. Maybe there's a phone outage."

Ainsley shook her head. "All the phones would be out."

"You're right. It's Skary. There's one line that runs through the entire town."

"Which means," Ainsley said, "that Wolfe doesn't care." She sniffled.

Melb sucked in a deep breath. "Ainsley, I rarely say this out loud, and never to myself, but maybe…maybe we overreacted."

Ainsley cut her eyes to Melb. "There's no mistaking what happened, Melb. And now this is confirming what I feared. We're too much trouble. Wolfe would rather be off doing some stupid play."

"Ainsley, I know one thing. Wolfe loves you and that baby more than life itself."

Ainsley's hot stare focused ahead as she sipped her equally hot coffee. "Then he's going to have to prove it."

CHAPTER 14

> Where angels might have sat enthroned, devils lurked, and glared out menacing.

IT WAS MIDAFTERNOON by the time "All right, I'll go" actually came to pass and Alfred went. He couldn't quite figure out how to put it to this woman. He supposed the best approach was to be vague and only answer questions that he had to. Still, he had to come up with a good reason why a grown man needed to see sock puppets, plus Tiny Tim, while remaining uncreepy.

So he decided to attempt charm and put on the appearance that this was a normal thing to do and that there was nothing odd or weird about it at all. He'd simply insert himself into the situation by way of association: he was merely tying up loose ends, making sure that everybody had everything they needed for the play.

He would then firmly look those two puppets right in their plastic eyes. After that, he would chat it up with Tiny Tim and practice good old-fashioned forgiveness.

Fifteen minutes later, he would be out the door and freed from the "redrum" of all hauntings.

The first sign that his plan might go awry was the fact that he found Katelyn Downey at home, in her pajamas, blotting her eyes as she answered the door. Her nose glowed bright red.

"May I help you?"

"Perhaps now is not a good time," he said, stepping backward.

"No, no. Please. Ignore...this." She gestured toward her face. "It's just been a bad morning. But I'm fine." She forced a smile.

"Okay...well, I wanted to stop by and check on the, uh, puppets."

Her eyes widened enough that Alfred wondered if he'd somehow, unbeknownst to him, accidentally thrown in an insult.

"The puppets?"

"I can come back." Alfred quickly turned, but she raced out the door and grabbed him by the arm.

"Wait. Please." She pulled him back to the porch. "I'm sorry. It just caught me by surprise, that's all. You're Alfred, right? The man who passed out last night? Are you okay?"

Well, at least he'd moved on from being the infamously failed editor and agent of Wolfe Boone. "I'm here at the request of Lois," he said, hoping that would add to the legitimacy of all this, "to inspect the puppets."

Tears squirted out of her eyes as she lowered her head and started blotting her face again.

"Um...I'm sorry, did I...?"

She shook her head. "No, please. Come in. Please."

"No, I don't think now's a good—"

"I insist." She opened the door wide and flagged him in with the tissue.

Alfred, against his better judgment, walked through the door.

The house had a more contemporary feel than the rest of the homes in Skary. It wasn't "cozy." Instead, it had updated paint, streamlined furniture, and, with a little help, some real lighting possibilities.

"I was just making some cider," she said. Alfred noticed a pot on the stove, with cloves and cinnamon floating on the top. Cider from scratch? She'd been indoctrinated. She dipped some out with a ladle, handed it to him in a Pier One mug, and asked him to join her at the Pottery Barn breakfast table. At least she had style. "This play," she said, waving her arms in the air like she was referring to an astronomical phenomenon, "has just taken over my life. I volunteered, you know, since I have experience in theater. Well, children's theater. Church children's theater. But anyway, I volunteered. Lois signed me up to make the hideous children, Ignorance and Want."

Alfred shivered.

"Then she asked if Willem might be able to do Tiny Tim. And I thought, 'Well, why not?' We've always known Willem is gifted, and he's got the good looks of a movie star, so we agreed he should do it. So on top of sewing these puppets, I've had to help Willem with his lines." She sighed as she rested her chin in her hand. "It's been overwhelming. And then last night, Lois was very disappointed with what I came up with. I don't think we're seeing eye-to-eye." She dabbed the corner of her eye.

Okay, well, that solved the mystery of why she couldn't stop crying. "May I...see the puppets?"

"She's checking up on me, isn't she?"

"No, no. Not at all. It's just procedure." Alfred tried to say that with an even expression. "Maybe I could... Maybe I could offer some suggestions."

Katelyn seemed to be motivating herself, and then she stood, left the room, and returned clutching a sack. She was about to open it when a little boy appeared in the doorway leading into the living room.

"Mommy, what's going on?" His gaze fixed on Alfred, who tried to look pleasant even though he wasn't a fan of children.

"Nothing, honey. This is just a man working with the play. Mr. Alfred. Can you say hello?"

Apparently not. And Alfred would prefer not to be called "Mr. Alfred" anyway.

"Willem here has been practicing very hard on his lines, haven't you, honey?"

Stare.

Katelyn cleared her throat. "Oh, now, Willem, let's not lead the nice Mr. Alfred here into thinking you've got stage fright." She glanced at Alfred. "He really doesn't. He's a very talkative child. Usually."

"It's okay."

"No, I insist. He must say his lines. You're here, after all, for that very purpose, aren't you?"

"Well, I did want to see Tiny Tim, but—"

"Willem! Say your lines this instant!"

Alfred waved his hand. "Mrs. Downey, please. It's not necessary. I'm sure this fine son of yours will rise to the occasion when it's time."

With a longsuffering expression, she gazed at her son as if he'd personally insulted her. Then the dryer buzzed, and she sprang up from the table. "Excuse me. I have to attend to that or, well, things wrinkle and..." Her voice trailed off into what looked to be another round of crying as she raced from the room.

Alfred glanced at the boy, who crossed his arms and frowned. "What did you do to my mother?"

"Me? Nothing. She was crying when I answered the door."

"No, she wasn't."

"Look, I think your mom is just a little stressed about this play, that's all." He hoped this was the right tone in which to speak to a child. He didn't have much experience.

"Why are you here?"

"Well, I'm uh...uh..." He gestured toward the bag that held the puppets, which sat in the middle of the table. "I'm just here to inspect the puppets. Do you like puppets?"

"Why would a grown man want to see puppets?"

"I...I don't *want* to see them. I just...well, look, it's complicated—"

"I bet." His eyes narrowed.

"Look, kid, beat it, okay?"

"And leave you alone with these puppets? I don't think so."

"Aren't you supposed to be Tiny Tim? Likable? Affable? Good-natured?"

"Terminal."

Alfred was about to retort when Katelyn returned, this time with fresh makeup and a gleaming smile. "Sorry about that. But there's nothing worse than ironing sheets." She smiled at her son, who returned the favor with an innocent, wide-eyed look in need of affirmation. "Oh, all right. Go ahead and go," she said with a wink.

But then he stepped forward, clasped his hands behind his back like he'd just morphed into a von Trapp, and said, *"God bless us, every one!"*

Katelyn clapped her hands together, gasping and gushing so

much she failed to notice the evil, sinister glance the kid gave Alfred. It diminished as he smiled angelically at his mother.

"I knew you could do it!"

"Can I play my Wii now?"

"Sure."

Before Alfred could even reconcile himself to the fact that he'd not forgiven Tiny Tim even the least bit and instead loathed him even more, Katelyn drew a puppet from the bag, and it stared him down.

Well, that wasn't really true. Each eye pointed outward so it couldn't look *right* at him. Its hair, brown, short, and stringy, stuck to the sock in an oddly meticulous pattern. Its mouth, bright red and crooked, gave him a preschool look. Alfred smiled, then laughed, slapping his hand on the table. "Ha. Ha-ha! He's not scary. He's not scary at all!"

"I know. I'm so sorry. The gummy worms didn't work. But I'm not sure what else to do."

"May I see Want?"

Katelyn pulled her out of the bag. Her hair, also long and stringy, was tied up with two bows on each side of her head, but that was the only difference. She looked exactly like Ignorance, gummy worms and all. Katelyn looked in desperate need of suggestions.

"Okay, well, maybe we can add some…slime."

"Slime?"

"Sure. Hanging off their faces." Katelyn didn't look inspired. "You've got a son. Surely he can help you acquire some slime."

She nodded and her eyes brightened. "I think you're right."

"And maybe lose the eyes. Cut holes out so they look empty."

"Oh, that is good!"

"That paired with a mouth that looks like it came off a crazed clown, and I think you'll be fine."

"Thank you, Alfred!"

"My pleasure." Alfred stood and glanced at the puppets one more time. With a chuckle, he shook his head and went to the door. "You'll do just fine."

"What about Willem? Do you think he'll do well?"

"Oh…sure. He brings a real immaturity to the role."

She placed a grateful hand on her heart. Alfred wanted to do the same because he thought, and was almost sure, that he would not fear Want or Ignorance anymore.

CHAPTER 15

> It was shrouded in a deep black garment, which concealed its head, its face, its form, and left nothing of it visible, save one outstretched hand. But for this it would have been difficult to detach its figure from the night, and separate it from the darkness by which it was surrounded.

IN THE WEE HOURS of the morning, when the entire community of Skary was asleep, Wolfe lay in bed contemplating irony. He liked irony—had used it a lot in his books. But living it was a different matter entirely. Like the way he was alone in the house, not a sound to be heard, but he couldn't sleep. No crying baby. No nagging wife. No visitors calling in the middle of the night. But he couldn't sleep.

Most of his wakeful time, he spent conversing inside his head with Ainsley about how wrong she was. It was a very one-sided conversation, but he didn't care. He was still angry. And, admittedly, heartbroken. They'd never had a fight like this. There had been a squabble or two, but nothing that wasn't resolved quickly.

He rose from bed before even Goose and Bunny awoke. He clicked on the television to eat his bowl of cold cereal. He was used to a nice big breakfast, so this was just another painful jab. Oliver hurried out the door without a word, presumably late to work.

Wolfe spent a while working on his book, the one that he'd decided might take him a lifetime to finish, and the rest of the morning working on his character for the play. The hours dragged on and on. He decided to pass the afternoon reading *A Christmas Carol.* He practically knew it by heart, usually reading it through at least once every Christmas. Of course, that was before Ainsley put the joy and holiday back into Christmas for him. Now he had parties and dinners and gift shopping. He volunteered at the church to bring food and toys to needy families. He helped decorate the community center.

The phone didn't ring one time, no matter how long he watched it and prayed it would. Even more gut-wrenching, it was all because he hadn't put the Christmas lights up.

Anger stirred all over again.

So the cycle went until evening, at which time Wolfe arrived at the theater. He'd been looking forward to this day. Of all the ghosts, he thought he would like to play this one, the Ghost of Christmas Yet To Come. Without a single word uttered, this ghost commanded fear in every reader's heart. Each time Wolfe read the first lines in the chapter that introduced the ghost, chills would race up and down his spine. He'd learned the valuable lesson that less is more, and used the technique often in his own books.

Wolfe entered from stage left, but nobody was around. "Hello?"

"Be there in a sec!" Lois called from behind the stage. The erected set looked pretty good. Painted on one panel was a gravesite, and on the other half of the stage was the Cratchits' living room with a fireplace, chairs, a throw rug, and a candlestick. Soon the other actors started arriving, including Oliver.

"Heard anything?" Wolfe asked him.

"I tried calling. Twice. She hung up both times."

"What are we supposed to do, then?"

"I don't know. It sure made for a long day."

"You know what? Two can play at this game."

"Four."

"The point is, if they're not going to tell us what's wrong, then why should we have to beg for the answers?"

"Because I miss breakfast."

"Me too."

"A lot."

"But we have to stay strong. Our stomachs cannot control us. They're the ones who are mad. They at least owe us an explanation."

"Sausage and biscuits…"

"Get ahold of yourself, Oliver. We can't cave."

"Not even for french toast?"

"All right, people! Gather around," Lois said, patting her hands together. "Tonight we're going to run the last of the scenes with the ghosts. Personally, this is one of my favorites. And not just because I play Mrs. Cratchit and have all the good lines!" She turned to them and took on her character. *"The Founder of the Feast indeed! I wish I had him here. I'd give him a piece of my mind to feast upon, and I hope he'd have a good appetite for it!"* Bowing to the light applause, Lois said, "That's the kind of energy I want from all of you. We're not in costume yet, but Wolfe, I would like to see you for a moment. There are a few things I want to fit you for. The rest of you, run your lines until we return. Wolfe, follow me."

Wolfe trailed behind Lois to the back of the stage. "Did you find a good black robe?"

"Find one? I made it myself. Stayed up all night sewing it. And by the way, it's deep plum."

"Purple?"

"If I'd meant purple, I would've said purple. It's deep plum."

"It's supposed to be black."

"Plum is more intriguing."

"It's right in the book," Wolfe said. *"It was shrouded in a deep black garment, which concealed its head, its face and—"*

Lois pulled the garment from a chest and whirled around to look at Wolfe. "It's an impressive talent that you can quote Dickens. It's just not going to come in handy in this play, all right?"

Wolfe folded his arms together. "Well, at least this ghost has no lines for you to butcher."

"Testy, aren't we?" She handed him the robe, and he held it up. It was dark enough that most people probably wouldn't notice it wasn't black. And it did have a hood. "We've got a lot of work to do on you before we get started. This ghost should be the scariest of them all. Which is why I've taken a bit of a liberty and expanded his...traits."

"What are you talking about? I extend my hand, make my finger look long, bony, and creepy."

She held up an eyeball hanging from a socket. "This, for one. I figure you can throw back your hood at the cemetery. It's going to draw quite a scream, I can assure you."

Wolfe hurried after her as she pushed through the curtain. "Lois, the phantom never takes off his hood! He is shrouded the entire time!"

"You know, Wolfe, that's the problem with you. You have no

vision. I'm simply adding an artistic element here, and you're having a cow."

"Lois, the entire idea is that this phantom, the one that delivers death to his doorstep, is quietly subdued. He's the darkness of the night, you see?"

"No, Wolfe, *you* see. And that's the problem. You can only see your way."

"Lois, I promise. I'm not trying to be artistically stubborn. I just want you to understand that more than physically scary, these ghosts are representative, symbolic of the sin and sadness of Ebenezer Scrooge. By focusing on the physical appearance of the ghosts, I'm afraid we're going to mislead the audience. They're going to miss the message. What is scarier than the spirits is Scrooge's eternal destiny."

His fellow actors listened attentively to their conversation while looking busy. Lois whipped around and pointed a finger into Wolfe's face. "You know what, Wolfe? You're like lip gloss on a windy day."

"Lip gloss?"

"Lip gloss is terrific, spectacular, even a little sexy, until there's wind. Then it becomes a nightmare. See what I'm getting at? I'm the lip gloss, and you're the windbag."

"I thought I was the lip gloss."

"Jealousy doesn't become you, Wolfe. Not everyone can be the lip gloss. Nobody else here has a problem with this play. Just you. Unless I get some sort of sign that I shouldn't do this play as is, I'm going forward with it—with or without you."

The stage fell silent. Everyone stared at Wolfe. As much as he wanted to detach himself from this horrific slaughter of a masterpiece, he wasn't about to lose his pride and drop out of the play. Not for a second.

"Fine. Have it your way."

"All right. Now, everyone, in your places. And Wolfe, get to the dressing room and secure your vampire teeth."

Alfred snapped his newspaper open as he sipped a latte. Evening had finally come, and the coffee shop was nearly empty. Every latte or green tea or dark roast he drank in this shop reminded him that miracles still happen. He remembered nearly weeping when they put the place in. And the cell phone tower that saved his sanity.

He'd managed to keep up appearances with a wide grin to everyone he met on the streets. He'd discovered it was all in the grin. A small smile or a half wave didn't cut it. You had to bare teeth. A sparkle in the eye didn't hurt either, which he achieved by tilting his head up a little and letting the streetlights hit his eyes.

Humming was out of the question for him, though he supposed he could pull it out of his proverbial holiday hat if need be. Short of that, it looked as if no Christmas intervention would be needed.

He could sit in quiet and peace, read his newspaper, drink something too expensive, and forget to be cheerful.

"Alfred?"

Alfred peeked over his paper. Ainsley. "Oh. Hello."

"What are you doing here so late in the evening? I figured you'd be at the theater along with everyone else."

It was only 8:30 p.m., but Alfred had learned a while back that this town's activity went down with the sun.

"My work is done with the play." He smiled.

"Mind if I join you?"

Alfred raised an eyebrow. "Why?"

"I need to talk." She plopped down in the other chair and threw off her coat. "Wolfe and I aren't speaking. I'm staying at Melb's."

Alfred folded his newspaper. "You seemed fine when I was over for dinner."

Ainsley shook her head, and her voice quivered. "I heard he's just doing this play so he can get out of the house. He doesn't want to be with me and Abigail."

"What? Ainsley, that's nonsense. He loves you both very much. When I see him, he blabs on and on about you two. Might I remind you he gave up his entire career for you? His whole life revolves around you."

"That's what I thought, but it's not true. I heard from someone in the cast that both Oliver and Wolfe are doing the play so they'll have something to do in the evenings."

Alfred didn't know what to say, except he couldn't blame them, but then again, he wasn't the domestic type.

"I'm sure there's a reasonable explanation."

"He hates this play. He says Lois is butchering it. The only reason he's there is to stay away from me."

Alfred reached across the table to take her hand. "There's not much I know about this world anymore, Ainsley. It used to be good to me, and now it's not. But one thing I'm sure of is that Wolfe's whole world would crumble if he lost you and Abigail. He loves you both with all his heart."

Tears dripped down her cheeks as she twisted her wedding ring around her finger. "I want to believe it."

"Then believe it."

"But how do you believe something that you can't see?"

Alfred squeezed her hand. "As your people like to say, 'Have faith.' "

CHAPTER 16

> "I understand you," Scrooge returned, "and I would do it, if I could. But I have not the power, Spirit. I have not the power."

"DID YOU SAY..." Martin cradled the phone in the crook of his neck as he jotted down notes. "*Two* tour buses full? No, no, that's just fine. Thank you. Um...parking, you say? Well, um, feel free to park in any empty field you see... Thank you. We'll look forward to seeing you." He hung up the phone and prepared himself for it to ring again. Thankfully there was a reprieve and he was able to catch his breath. He turned on the answering machine, which gave the performance times, and then bundled up in his coat as he headed outdoors. It was a rather short walk to the theater, and he hurried over, hoping to catch Lois.

He found her organizing a costume rack. "Lois."

She turned and smiled. "Hello, Martin. What are you doing here? We're not scheduled for a dress rehearsal right now." She tapped her finger on her lips. "By the way, I've been meaning to tell you, I like how you're playing Bob Cratchit. I really do. Understated. Happy. Noble. An everyday family guy. You've really put some thought into this."

"Oh, uh, thanks. Listen—"

Lois held up her hands and looked away. "Martin, I feared this would come up. I've been trying to handle it in the most sensitive way possible. I realize our playing husband and wife in the production is a bit awkward and most likely painful for you. But I want you to look on the bright side. At least you don't have to wear garlic."

"Lois, please. No need to apologize. I'm perfectly fine with the arrangement. I promise. I'm happy for you and the sheriff. You suit each other."

"That's kind of you to say."

"I came here to give you some news. I don't know if you realize, but people are coming to this production by the busload. Literally. Tour buses."

Lois's eyes grew wide. "For our little play?"

"Yes! We're blowing the competition away."

"What competition?"

"I can't quite put all the details together because I'm getting bits of information here and there, but apparently there's another play going on the exact same night we're performing ours."

Lois's enthusiasm dwindled.

"But, Lois, they're coming to *ours.* From what I understand, the other play is the nativity story. *Ours* is the one that's stirring up all the buzz." Martin held out his hand for Lois to shake. "I just can't thank you enough for what you're doing for this community, Lois. The theater is a hit. Not only are people coming from all around to see what we're doing, but our own citizens are rallying behind this. We've got people offering to bring cookies and hot chocolate for after the play, not to mention all the people doing costumes and playing the roles. It's a gift you have. And it's a gift for this town."

Lois's eyes glistened with emotion. "Martin, how kind of you to say so."

"I won't keep you. I know you've got a lot to do before the dress rehearsal."

"Then I will see you tomorrow night."

"Tomorrow? The dress rehearsal is tonight."

Lois blinked. "It is?"

"Yes." Martin studied Lois as she seemed to give this some thought.

"That makes sense," she finally said. "I didn't sleep last night." She waved her hand. "I'll be fine. Time to catch up on sleep later, right? I'm discovering I don't need as much sleep as I once thought. In fact, I think it helps my creative juices flow."

Martin left the theater filled with good cheer. He watched from the sidewalk as the residents of Skary scurried from one shop to the next. It was going to be a great Christmas. Maybe, just maybe, they'd be out of the red this year.

Wolfe had an hour to kill before Lois murdered Dickens, by way of dress rehearsal. Once again, he couldn't get over the irony. He played a ghost, yet his soul was as vexed as if he were Scrooge himself.

"Wolfe, what a pleasure to see you," Reverend Peck said as he stood from behind his desk. "Have a seat."

Wolfe sighed as he sat down, wondering how he would break the news to his pastor that his wife was staying elsewhere. This wasn't his proudest moment. The reverend had always been kind to him, since the first day he'd come to this church asking about God and what it all meant. They'd grown to be very good friends. Wolfe knew his trouble with his wife would likely test their friendship. The reverend remained close to Ainsley and her father.

"I didn't realize you'd be here so quickly."

"What?"

"I just left the message a few minutes ago. But this is just another sign, my friend. Another sign, by golly!" The reverend clapped his hands a couple of times as he hustled around his desk. "So you're probably wondering why I've called you here."

His cheeks turned ruddy from laughing. Wolfe couldn't help but feel relieved that the purpose of the meeting wasn't to admonish him. But he couldn't recall ever seeing the reverend so excitable.

"As you know," the reverend began, "it's Christmastime, and there's no escaping it in this town. There's a reminder at every corner, in every window, on every light post. And though I admire the enthusiasm of Skary, I've always tried my best to show them the true meaning of the season. This is the year, Wolfe! This is the year!"

"Why?"

"I heard from God. I mean, really heard from Him. He spoke to me, Wolfe. We're going to see a miracle in this town! I don't know what or when, but God is going to do something amazing!" The reverend's glee faded. "What's the matter?"

Wolfe rose and went to the window, where he stared out at the cold night sky. "It's just…it's just that…" He exhaled loudly. "So much is going wrong."

"Which means that God is going to do even bigger things!" The reverend jumped to his feet and joined Wolfe at the window. "You are troubled."

Wolfe glanced at him. "It's nothing."

"Nothing?"

"Many things." Wolfe stared out the window. Now wasn't a good time to talk about Ainsley. He didn't want to take away from the reverend's gusto. He shook his head a little. "It's just the play. I'm having a hard time swallowing Lois's interpretation."

"Oh?"

"Scrooge has been double-crossed by the government. I'm a mixed metaphor of a ghoul, thanks to a misplaced eyebrow, vampire teeth, and werewolf claws. Everything that Dickens meant for his book to be, it now isn't." Wolfe sighed. Dickens wasn't the only thing mixed up. His marriage was meant for more too.

The reverend put his arm around Wolfe's shoulder. "The truth has a way of coming out, my friend."

Wolfe checked his watch. "So why did you call me here?"

"Let's pray, Wolfe. Let's pray that nothing will stop God's miracle. Let's pray that God would open the hearts of every person in Skary to see the great thing He is going to do."

"Sure, Reverend," Wolfe replied, "and can we say a prayer for Charles Dickens?"

"Isn't he dead?"

"Well, you might actually see someone rise from the dead this weekend."

CHAPTER 17

The Ghost conducted him through several streets familiar to his feet; and as they went along, Scrooge looked here and there to find himself, but nowhere was he to be seen.

HAD WOLFE BEEN ABLE to staple his tongue down, he would've. He walked the corridors and observed the cast getting ready for their one and only dress rehearsal, trying to keep his mouth shut.

Lois flitted around like a stage goddess, actually wearing a scarf that hung down to her knees and bifocals that weren't even real. That was, of course, before she changed into Mrs. Cratchit, who looked more like Mrs. Brady.

Playing with the eyeball that dangled by a metal coil from his face, he watched the first act, which, in full costume, was an even bigger disaster.

Dustin, who played Fred, Scrooge's infinitely optimistic nephew, seemed to be capturing the character in short spurts. One moment he'd brim with enthusiasm and the next, fall flat as a pancake, then bounce back with misplaced anger. But Fred was the least of the play's concerns.

Scrooge was having an identity crisis, what with the many "creative liberties" that Lois had taken with the dialogue. Although Oliver was doing his best to focus, he went from sounding like a fanatic to actually drawing quite a bit of pity, especially with the fainting scene Lois had written in, where Scrooge discovers he might have fathered a child out of wedlock. Of course, he hasn't—the Ghost of Christmas Past is just making a clever joke and somehow trying to prove a point, beyond what Dickens imagined in the scene where Belle chastises Scrooge for erecting the idol of Gain. In Lois's version, it played out like a bad soap opera, with Belle slapping Scrooge and kicking him where it counts before leaving him for a younger man with a Roth IRA.

The only thing that truly worked in the entire first act was the ghost, played by the sheriff. Dickens described him as both childlike and old, and unfortunately for the aging sheriff, the dumbstruck expression on his face, along with the fact that he kept tugging at the bottom of his costume, helped him nail that look.

Then Wolfe had to suffer through the second act. When Scrooge touches the Ghost of Christmas Present's robe, he is supposed to be transported into town, where a merry, bustling crowd of people are enjoying the cheer of Christmas. But in a way only a sleep-deprived Stepaphanolopolis could dream up, she'd decided to show the true nature of crowd shoppers and throw in a squabble over a Farrah Fawcett-Majors doll, which they all learned had scarred Lois when she was the only kid in town who didn't have one. Hers was ripped from her mother's arms on Christmas Eve by a father of twins, right in the middle of the toy store. The Ghost of Christmas Present goes on to sprinkle the violent crowd with water, and they disperse, but not before scarring every Dickens admirer that ever lived.

Lois did manage to keep the Cratchit scene somewhat intact, though she insisted that Mrs. Cratchit should be the focal point. After all, a woman holds the home together, and Tiny Tim shouldn't be a scene stealer. Which might have been the way to go, since Willem Downey did a poor job evoking any sort of sympathy.

Wolfe watched Oliver and Garlic Garth observe the Cratchits in their living room, cozy around the fire, loving one another, despite all that had gone wrong in their life. He couldn't help but think of Ainsley and Abigail. Was his cause enough of a reason to refuse to call? Why was he being so stubborn? It wasn't really in his nature, though he'd been more that way before he'd come down the hill and been transformed by a faith he had known little about.

He was sure that any minute she would walk through the doors, apologize for leaving, explaining why and asking for his forgiveness. But the minutes had turned into hours, and the hours into days. Now it seemed nobody would give in. Having them away did nothing for his sleep deprivation.

Still, his couldn't hold a candle to Lois's, which seemed to account for what appeared to be random acts of hallucination. Sleep deprived or not, Lois had managed to see her dream through… *A Christmas Carol* was now truly a horror.

"Isn't this delightful?" Alfred stepped up beside him in his sleek black trench coat, his hair slicked back like he used to wear it. He pulled off his shiny leather gloves as he watched the play.

"Isn't what delightful?" Wolfe asked, after dropping the vampire teeth out of his mouth.

"This!" Alfred said, gesturing toward the stage. "It's going to be a smashing success!"

"It's crushing, I'll give it that."

Alfred cut his gaze sideways. "Oh, now, Wolfe, don't be such a Scrooge."

"Funny." Wolfe turned to him and lowered his voice. "How can you approve of this whole thing?"

"You haven't been to New York in a long time, Wolfe. Things are irreverently portrayed at every stop on Broadway. The more irreverent, the better. Though I must admit, I've seen nudity, but I've not seen garlic."

"You're a purist, Alfred. Ever since I've known you."

"Yes, well, who says you can't teach an old dog new tricks, Wolfe? I've learned to embrace Skary, Indiana, so why not embrace its unconventional portrayal of the classics too? In case you haven't noticed, this sort of 'fits.' "

"But there's a twinkle in your eye, and I'm willing to bet it's not because you're going on a sleigh ride."

Alfred laughed. "True, but don't let that get out. There's a rumor spreading that I might've co-written 'Jingle Bells,' and let's just say it's only helping my cause."

"What cause?"

"You haven't heard? People are coming in droves to see this play."

"What are you talking about?"

"Tour buses, senior citizen centers, families of fifteen. We may run out of seats! All because I," he said, gesturing grandly toward himself, "can market *anything.* Don't look so surprised. Someone had to sell you to the editorial board all those years ago. I remember several who thought you didn't have a strong enough writing style and that you couldn't carry off a metaphor if your life depended on it. I sold you then, and I've sold this now. People are coming, simply because I said they should."

Wolfe folded his arms and scowled at Garth plugging his nostrils with each index finger as he tried to deliver his lines.

"You're in a sour mood," Alfred observed with a wry smile. "Is it because your eye fell out of its socket?"

"I have reason to be. More than one reason to be."

"Ainsley?"

"How do you know that?"

Alfred held up his hands. "I don't want to butt in. Besides, this is my night to be cheerful. I am going to be cashing in on this production without having to take responsibility for it. What better place can a man be in?"

The lights went down, and the actors scuttled offstage. Wolfe noticed Oliver and tried to give him a reassuring smile, but instead, Oliver tucked his chin into his shoulder and scooted between him and Alfred without a word. This wasn't the first time tonight Wolfe noticed Oliver avoiding him. He followed Oliver into the dressing room, hoping to give him some encouragement. He figured his own negativity was affecting Oliver, and perhaps he felt badly about his performance. But the truth be told, Oliver was the only thing saving this show. He'd really come into his own and grasped the character of Scrooge and his government conspiracies.

"You've really surprised me, Oliver," he said from the doorway as Oliver adjusted his top hat. "You've obviously put a lot of thought into what you've done."

Oliver turned, his eyes wide.

"I'm sorry, I didn't mean to startle you. I just wanted to—"

"Don't judge me! You don't know what it's been like!"

"Oliver, I'm not judging you. I know this has been difficult. I'm sorry I gave you that impression." He sighed and entered the dressing room. "Apparently, I'm the only one with the problem."

Relief overcame Oliver's face. "You should tell her that. It would mean a lot."

"Trust me, Oliver. She won't listen."

"That's what I thought, but then I talked to her, and we got on the same page."

"Yeah, well, she thinks I'm intentionally trying to be difficult, that I'm questioning her because I want to assert my expertise into the situation."

"No. You've got it all wrong. She thinks you're doing the play because you don't want to be around her and Abigail."

A long, strained silence passed between them, and with each second, Oliver's eyes grew wider, until a string of words came tumbling out of his mouth. "I, um, I mean...what's wrong...not wrong but you should...no, I should...it's just that..." Oliver sucked in a breath. "What were we talking about?"

"I was talking about Lois and the play." Wolfe crossed his arms and spread his feet into a stance. "What were you talking about?"

"Same thing."

"No, you weren't."

"Yes, I was."

"No, you weren't. You were talking about Ainsley and Abigail."

Oliver gave a pathetic shrug and a heavy sigh as he gazed at the floor. "I went back to Melb."

"What? I thought we agreed we were going to stand our ground!"

"You agreed to that, Wolfe. But I couldn't hang on. I felt terrible about what I did."

"What did you do?"

"I had no idea, but it must've been something terrible." Oliver glanced up at him. "And it was." He bit his lip. "Dustin inadvertently spilled the beans to them. He'd heard us talking about why we were doing this play—to get out of the house. They took it really personally, like we didn't want to be around them. I tried to explain that it wasn't that we didn't want to be around them. We just didn't want to be around baby poop."

Wolfe slowly sank onto the bench near the door. "Ainsley thinks I don't want to be around her? And the baby?"

"I tried as best I could to convince her otherwise, Wolfe. But I sort of had my hands full with Melb. She took me back in, and I can only be thankful. I begged and pleaded and promised to do whatever it took to get her back." Oliver gulped. "Let's just say she took me up on that offer. But at least I'm back home and with my family."

"How can she think that?" Wolfe asked. "That I don't want to be with her and Abigail?"

"They can't separate the poop like we can. To them, the diaper and the baby are one." Oliver stepped closer to Wolfe and put his hand on his shoulder. "I'll be honest with you, friend. Ainsley is desperately upset. It didn't help matters that I came groveling back before you did. You're going to have to think long and hard about what you can say to convince her to come home." He went to the door. "I'm sorry I wasn't stronger. But at the end of the day, I just wanted my family back. I couldn't go another day without them."

He left. Wolfe stood, walked to the sink, and looked in the mirror. He was hardly recognizable with the dangling eye and the blood dripping from the corner of his mouth. But he suspected that even without the makeup, he'd have a hard time recognizing who he'd become over the last few days. Pride had swallowed his compassion. If he'd just gone to talk to Ainsley the first night, it could've all been resolved. But now it had become something bigger, and he knew he'd really hurt his wife.

"Wolfe!" Lois's voice screeched through the backstage. "Wolfe?"

Wolfe emerged from the dressing room and stepped right in front of Lois, who stopped and planted her fists atop her hips. "What are you doing? Where are your vampire teeth? And why do you look like you're about to cry?"

Wolfe glanced away. "Just getting into character."

Lois paused. "I like it. An overly emotional ghost. Yeah, keep it, but don't go overboard. We can't have your makeup smearing. Now, get onstage! It's your cue!"

Luckily, he didn't have any lines, because the only words going through his head were the ones he hoped would win his wife and daughter back.

CHAPTER 18

> The Spirit stopped; the hand was pointed elsewhere.
>
> "The house is yonder," Scrooge exclaimed. "Why do you point away?"
>
> The inexorable finger underwent no change.

WITH A STABBING HEADACHE and a tired body, Wolfe rose out of bed, skipped a breakfast of what would've just been toast, took the dogs for a quick walk, and then headed for Oliver and Melb's house. He'd spent most of the night and into the early morning trying to figure out how to explain everything to Ainsley. It wasn't quite as simple as a misunderstanding, because he had indeed taken the role to get some time out of the house. But how could he make her understand that it didn't mean that he didn't love her or want to be around Abigail?

The words and the explanation weren't coming easily, so he decided to get a couple of hours sleep—he did, after all, have a play to perform tonight—and then go talk to her. He rang the doorbell at the Stepaphanolopolises' house, hoping little Ollie wasn't asleep.

Oliver answered with a plate full of breakfast items, including sausage. Something bulged in his cheek. "Woof?" He quickly chewed and swallowed. "Wolfe, what are you doing here?"

"I came to talk to Ainsley."

Suddenly Melb was at the door, not looking happy. "What are you doing here?"

"He came to talk to Ainsley," Oliver said, stuffing bacon into his mouth. "Hey, why don't you come in? We've got a ton of breakfast left over. You could—"

"I don't think so," Melb said, stepping in front of Oliver. "You're a little late."

"Look, I'm not here to eat breakfast. I want to talk to Ainsley."

"That's what I said. You're a little late. She's not here."

"Then where can I find her?"

Melb's eyes narrowed. "I don't know, Wolfe. Don't you think it's a little late to be coming back now?"

"Oliver came back just yesterday."

"No. Oliver crawled back and begged for mercy." Oliver sheepishly chewed his food and glanced away. "You don't look like you're crawling."

"Melb, with all due respect, I think this is between me and Ainsley. Now, please step aside. I would like to talk to her."

"You can't. She's not here. When Oliver came back she felt like she was intruding. I tried to convince her to stay, but she wouldn't. She took Abigail and left this morning."

"Where did she go?"

"I don't know. She wouldn't say."

A desperate urgency climbed through his body as he tried to think it through.

"Try her dad's house," Melb said. The eagerness in her eyes betrayed the flat tone of her voice. She gave a small, encouraging smile and then shut the door.

Wolfe lingered on the porch, sniffing the smell of bacon.

Back in New York, Alfred was accustomed to rising at 6:00 a.m. He often worked sixteen-hour days and most of the time didn't mind it. The energy of the city revived him when he got tired.

In Skary, however, he found himself sleeping in until ten many mornings. Most of the stores didn't even open until then, with the exception of the coffeehouse, thankfully. He had often tried to stay on a respectable schedule, but sleep found a way of drowning out all the regrets and failures he had to face when awake.

This morning, however, he rose before six, made himself a big breakfast, then opened his laptop and read the *New York Times,* the *New Yorker,* and the *Boston Globe.* It was going to be a good day! Hordes of people would be filtering into Skary by late afternoon. Alfred guessed it might be standing room only. Perhaps they would even have to turn people away. Whatever the case, it was sure to be a success.

As he sipped some orange juice, he noticed a strange sound outside. At first, he just thought it was the wind, but as he listened more carefully, he realized it was one of the strangest sounds he'd ever heard. He set his orange juice down and went to his front door, pressing his ear against it.

"What *is* that?"

He didn't have a peephole, but he did have a small front window. Still, he couldn't see his porch very well. But then something moved, and he barely caught sight of it. It looked gray. He hurried back to his door and listened again. It was something...*alive.* He could hear it breathing, or maybe it was his own breathing, which had grown increasingly panicked.

It sounded like...

Alfred swung open the door, yelped and jumped back, drawing his hands toward his face to cover up the awful smell that lurched toward him.

"A donkey?" Alfred muttered. The beast stood perfectly still, peacefully blinking every so often and flicking its tail. "A *donkey*?" How in the world had a donkey come to his front door?

He noticed a man walking with a cane down the sidewalk. He was almost out of sight, but Alfred saw a rope hanging from his arm. The donkey nearly blocked the entire doorway, but Alfred managed to squeeze by it and chase after the man. "Hey! *Hey!* You! Stop right there! *Stop!*"

The man turned and waited. Alfred suddenly noticed he still wore his pajamas and house slippers. Thankfully he had a robe on too, which he abruptly tightened around himself. Catching his breath, he asked, "Did you just leave a donkey on my doorstep?"

Wrinkles crisscrossed the man's skin like the top of a peanut butter cookie. He was nearly bald and couldn't stand up straight. But his eyes, youthful and sparkling, told a different story. "Yes sir, I did."

"Why?"

"You're Alfred Tennison, are you not?"

"I am."

"Well, sir, you've got a noble cause going, and I wanted to help. It's just a small thing, you know. I don't have much. But I know the good Lord can take the smallest of things and use them to His glory."

Alfred wasn't sure what to say because he wasn't following the conversation very well.

"What am I supposed to do with a donkey?"

"It's for your play."

"First of all, it's not my play. Secondly, why would I need a donkey?"

The old man lifted his gaze toward Alfred's house where the donkey still stood. "His name is Isaiah. I've had him for many years. He's been a good friend. But he's getting old now, just like me. His last days could be used for something wonderful."

Alfred realized the old man must be suffering from dementia. He put a gentle hand on the man's shoulder and tried a calmer voice. "As much as I appreciate your thoughtfulness, to be honest, sir, we're not using any animals."

"Not using any animals? How can that be? Everyone is talking about what a big production this is going to be, something we'll never, ever forget."

Alfred raised an eyebrow. "Well, um, sure. It's definitely going to be...unforgettable. But there are no animals in this story."

The man managed to stand more upright as he pushed on his cane. "Well, how do they get to Bethlehem? And what, exactly, is going to be in the stable?"

"The stable?"

"You're not having a stable either? Well, at least tell me there's going to be wise men."

A cold fear froze all the words on Alfred's tongue.

The old man shook his head. "I just thought perhaps he could carry Mary. Or at the very least be near the manger. He's been a good old donkey, I tell you. What a way for him to go out, you know?"

"Sir, are you certain we are talking about the same thing? This is Skary, and we're producing a play tonight, but it's not a Christmas pageant."

The man's eyes went wide. "Of course it is. People have been talking nonstop about this. Nobody has performed a Christmas pageant around here in years. We're all looking forward to it. My entire family is coming. That is twenty-five people, sir, including three great-grandchildren."

"But...but there's been a... It's not...but it's..."

"Yes?"

Alfred desperately looked around, as if help might be nearby. How could this have happened? "How many people, would you say, are expecting the pageant?"

"Everyone!"

A small yelp escaped, even as Alfred tried to compose himself. How could he not have seen this coming? Sure, news traveled fast in this part of the country, but he'd forgotten to factor in how quickly and often the facts get lost en route. A curse word slid to the front of the line and jumped out of his mouth before he could stop it. "I...I, uh...I need to..."

The man stopped him. "Son, listen to me. I'm no expert on theatrical productions, but I can tell you, stick with the story. Don't try to be innovative and leave out the stable. It will ruin the whole thing. Tell it like it's supposed to be told. It's rich and beautiful, and there's no need to tamper with it. Now, I must go." He looked at Isaiah, still at Alfred's doorstep. "He'll be a good donkey for you. He's as gentle as they come and hardly has a stubborn bone in his body, which is unusual for a donkey. He'll do fine for you."

The old man turned and walked off. But Alfred couldn't move. The donkey, still swishing its tail from side to side, seemed the perfect visual for Alfred's predicament. In fact, not too long from now, he imagined people would be seeing him as a donkey, as well.

Wolfe stood with his hands clasped in front of him as the sheriff's unhappy expression greeted him. "Wolfe."

"Look, I just wanted to—"

"I don't want to hear it, Wolfe. You're making her an emotional wreck, causing her to doubt everything. I realize that you're meaning no harm, but this is her life, Wolfe. It means so much to her, and to have you dismiss it like it's a joke—"

"I don't mean to interrupt, sir, but I have to tell you that it's really just been a big misunderstanding. Yes, I did decide to do the play so I could have time out of the house. But that hasn't changed my commitment. I promise."

"I think you should tell her that. It would mean a lot."

"Is she here?"

"Here? No, she's at the theater."

"The theater? She's probably looking for me, isn't she?"

"Not that I know of. But I think it would be a good move to go and reassure her now, while you can. Tonight is going to get very busy, as you know. She could use some encouragement."

Wolfe let out a hopeful smile. "Sir, I plan to do much more than encourage her. I plan to apologize more than I've ever apologized to anyone before. And I am going to take her into my arms, hug her and kiss her until she begs me to stop."

The sheriff suddenly looked mortified. "I believe a simple apology will suffice."

"It's just that she means the world to me, Sheriff. I adore her. I love her more than I can express."

"What are you talking about?" the sheriff's voice boomed. "You should be in love with your wife!"

"I am in love with my wife! Who did you think I was talking about?"

"Lois!"

"Lois?"

"Why are you acting this way? You just told me you would go and apologize to her for the way you've been acting with this play. What does Ainsley have to do with this?"

"Um…" The words trailed off as the sheriff glared hard at him.

"Well?"

"We just got into a little fight, that's all."

"A fight? Then why are you here?"

"I thought she might be staying here."

"You mean she's not staying with you?"

"No."

He folded his arms. "What did you do?"

"It was just a misunderstanding. Ainsley thought I didn't want to be around her and the baby."

"Why would she think that?"

"She heard I decided to do the play to get some time away."

"Well, that's just absurd. Why would she think that?"

Wolfe bit his lip. "I, uh…"

"It's true?"

"No...yes, I mean...it's complicated."

The sheriff stepped forward. "If you know what's good for you, you'll get your tail out of here and go find your wife. And here's what you say. You tell her how sorry you are, and you reassure her that your family is your whole world. You explain that sometimes you feel incompetent as a father—that you watch her mother your daughter and you wish you could do it with as much grace. You tell her that sometimes you feel overwhelmed by the situation, but it doesn't mean you don't love them. Apologize to her for not coming and talking about it and instead choosing to be a moron."

Wolfe sort of wished he had a pen and paper to jot some notes down. "Oh, good. That sounds good. I've been having a hard time figuring out what to say."

"She'll forgive you. I promise."

"How do you know?"

He grinned. "Because a long time ago, I did the very same thing."

CHAPTER 19

He took a little child and set him in the midst of them.

MARK 9:36

WITH THE DONKEY in tow, Alfred walked toward the theater, avoiding the glances from local residents. He led Isaiah through the front doors of the theater where he found people milling around getting the stage ready. It hurt his heart to even look at it. Pulling the donkey along, he walked down the aisle toward the stage. A ramp allowed Isaiah up onto the stage, where everyone stopped what they were doing to stare.

"I need Lois. Where is Lois?"

A man getting Scrooge's bed ready shrugged. "We haven't seen her since early this morning."

"What? Why?"

"Nobody knows."

Alfred glanced at Isaiah, who seemed to be watching everything he did. "Come on. Let's go look backstage."

For the most part, the backstage area was quiet. "Lois?" Alfred called, hopeful that perhaps she'd come in through the back door. "Lois? Are you here?" No one answered. But suddenly Isaiah began moving in the direction of the storage closets. "Isaiah. No. Whoa. Whoa." Apparently, that only worked for horses, because Isaiah didn't look like he had any intention of stopping. "Hey, now, come here, boy. Come on. You hungry? Is that it?"

Tugging Alfred along, Isaiah finally stopped in front of one of the doors. Sniffing it, he rubbed his forehead against the door. Alfred noticed it was slightly open. With gentle fingers, he slowly opened the door and peered into the dark room. He found the switch for the light bulb, and when he turned it on, he saw Lois curled up in the corner of the room, fast asleep.

"Lois!"

She startled awake, disoriented and panicked. "What? Where? No, I said a Swiss bank account not a Swiss accent, you idiot!"

"Lois, it's Alfred."

She blinked a few times, then looked up, just noticing him. "Why are you in the closet?" she asked.

"Why are you in here? You were asleep."

She glanced around. "No, I wasn't."

"Yes, you were."

"No, Alfred. I was simply… I was getting focused." She stood and adjusted her outfit. "Now, if you'll excuse me, I've got a lot to do for tonight. Is my hair okay?"

"It's fine. Lois, listen to me. I have to tell you something."

"Can't it wait?"

"No."

She looked at the donkey. "Well, if you were going to tell me you have a donkey with you, I can see that for myself. So if you'll excuse me."

"Lois," Alfred said, his voice trembling, "I don't know how to tell you this, so I'm just going to tell you. But before I do, I want you to know"—Alfred tried to hold back the emotion in his voice—"I take full responsibility for this."

"For what?"

"There's been a miscommunication." Alfred tried to gain the courage to say it aloud. "There are a lot of people coming tonight. But they think they're coming to see…"

"Yes?"

"A nativity play."

"A nativity play?"

"Yes. They're expecting the story of the birth of Jesus, complete with live animals."

Alfred carefully studied Lois for any reaction, but there was nothing. He couldn't be entirely sure she was even breathing. She simply stood there like she was in a trance. "Lois?"

Nothing. Frozen like a statue.

"Lois, listen, I was thinking about how we might resolve this. Maybe we could do a…a reading. Yes, that's perfect. After the show, somebody could stand up there and read the Christmas story from the Bible." Alfred paused as he watched Lois's lack of reaction. "I'll even do it, Lois. I'll stand up there and read it cover to cover. Or chapter to chapter. Whatever the case, I'll read it, and I can be quite dramatic when I want to be. I don't mention it much, but I once was hired to do the audio book of a very famous author. So what do you say?" Alfred paused, waiting. "Lois, please. Say something."

She finally snapped out of her trance and looked at him. "How did this happen? We had a flier printed up with all the information on it."

Alfred looked down. "I know. I didn't use them. I thought word of mouth might be a better way to go. And it worked perfectly. The news spread like wildfire. It's just that it was the wrong news."

Tears filled her eyes. "So everybody coming here tonight thinks they're going to see a nativity play?"

Alfred nodded solemnly. "But Lois, I'm sure they will love what you're doing. They will be just as happy once they see it."

"You don't understand, Alfred. Skary needs this. Mayor Blarty said this could really help us get out of the red this year! We can't disappoint people like this! We'll be a laughingstock!" She began to sob.

Alfred clutched the donkey's mane, trying to figure out what to do—how he could help. But the only thing clear was that he'd failed. Again. And this time, it would affect an entire town.

But as fast as she'd begun to sob, Lois stopped. She wiped the tears off her face, stood up straight, and pressed her lips into a determined, straight line. "All right. If that's what they want, that's what we'll give them."

"What are you talking about?"

"We are going to put on a nativity play." She turned toward the direction of the stage. "We have to."

"No...no, we don't!" Alfred pulled Isaiah along and trailed behind her as she headed for the stage. "Lois, you can't change a play in just a few hours! What are you thinking?"

"Life takes boldness, Alfred. Sometimes you have to do the bold thing."

"But...but it's never going to work! Lois, stop and think. You've got an entire set built. You've got costumes. What about lines? How is everyone going to know their lines?"

Lois clapped her hands and gathered everyone around. "People, listen to me. Stop what you're doing. I need you to go and find every cast member of this play. Be back in thirty minutes. We've got a very important meeting. Hustle! Go!"

Alfred's mouth hung open as he clutched the donkey's rope. Lois regarded him for a moment and then gave him a sly smile. "I told you that you should learn to read signs better. Alfred, this is a sign."

Ainsley held Abigail close to her chest as she sat quietly in the pew of the church. A light snow fell outside, and the room was chilly, since Reverend Peck could only afford to heat the place on Sundays. She'd tried to stay strong for Abigail and not cry in front of her. Though she was just a baby, Ainsley thought she would surely sense distress. According to Melb, Ainsley might scar her for life.

As Abigail napped, Ainsley prayed. She didn't want to stay mad at Wolfe, and she didn't want to feel bitter, but at the same time, she couldn't deny the truth. In some ways, it didn't seem possible, but she knew people changed, and maybe Wolfe had decided family life wasn't for him.

Doubts and fears swarmed her as she struggled to find peace. No matter what Wolfe decided, she knew God wouldn't abandon her. Her entire life, she'd always believed God was enough, but now she wondered how she could survive without Wolfe.

She heard someone walk in. Turning, she found Reverend Peck walking toward her. "Ainsley? I thought that was you. What are you doing here?"

That was all it took for the tears to flow. She sobbed and leaned into her pastor as he slid in the pew and wrapped an arm around her. "There, there," he said. "It's okay." He stroked Abigail's head and let Ainsley cry awhile. "Tell me what's the matter."

Ainsley explained it all the best she could, but even as it came out of her mouth, she found it hard to believe.

"Ainsley," the Reverend said gently, "Wolfe was just here today. He didn't mention a thing about it."

It wasn't even on his mind? She started sobbing all over again.

Wolfe had searched for Ainsley for an hour but still hadn't found her. She hadn't gone to the house, and she wasn't at the grocery store or the coffee shop. He'd even stopped by Dr. Hass's, but he hadn't seen her.

He came out of the doctor's office, deciding to check the church one more time, when he noticed Dustin walking rapidly toward him. "Wolfe! Hey! Hold on!"

"What's wrong?"

"Dude, you've got to get to the theater now. Lois is calling, like, this meeting."

"What for?"

"I don't know."

Wolfe walked with Dustin to the theater where everybody was streaming in single file. Oliver noticed him and waited. "What is this about?" Oliver asked.

"I don't know," Wolfe said, "but I don't have time for it. I'm trying to find Ainsley."

"You haven't found her?"

"No."

As they came into the theater, they noticed Lois onstage, flagging everyone toward her. "Come on, hurry up, people." Everyone took a seat. Wolfe noticed that Lois looked peculiar. She wasn't in hysterics, but by the expression on her face, it seemed she should be. She took a deep breath, waited till it was perfectly quiet, and then said, "We've got a problem."

For ten minutes, the theater was silent, except Lois, who explained something nobody could quite understand. She put it three or four different ways, but still, it was difficult to make any sense of.

The cast, led by Oliver, began peppering Lois with questions.

"Calm down! Everyone! Please!"

"I can't believe you're even saying this!" Wolfe said. "We've been working ourselves to death on this play. Everyone knows their lines. We're ready to roll. How can we possibly get an entirely new play together in just a few hours?"

Lois suddenly seemed calm. "First of all, we will do *A Christmas Carol.* It will simply be postponed. Why not for Valentine's? I bet no other theater has ever thought to do this as a non-Christmas play. Secondly, we all know the Christmas story. We're going to do an improvisational Christmas pageant. Again, unconventional. I once thought improv was irrelevant, but who wants to settle for being mainstream, people? We have a chance to show we can think outside the box..."

Suddenly Martin stepped forward. "Everyone, listen to me. I've been fielding calls for weeks about this. People are excited. They're coming by the busloads. We can't let them down. We've got to find a way to pull this thing off!"

"What about costumes?" somebody asked.

"Hey, like, we could use all the old stuff they had to wear at The Haunted Mansion. Turn some of those capes inside out, and you've got a shepherd's coat."

"And we could use the mummy costumes to wrap the baby," Garth said.

"What baby?" Wolfe asked.

"Ollie could play Jesus," Oliver offered.

"We could get hay pretty easily," the sheriff added.

Wolfe grabbed the sides of his head. "This is never going to work. Nobody here has ever done improv, Lois."

"Which means, simply, that there are no lines to drop. You'll go with the moment. We'll write out a basic outline, keep the set simple, and rely on everyone's emotional performances to carry this thing. Plus"—she smiled—"we've got a donkey. A real, live donkey. That's a sign, people. Don't you understand? This pageant is what we were supposed to do all along. Now," she said and then paused for a moment. "Does anybody have a Bible with them?"

"I can get one from the bookstore," Dustin offered.

"All right. Now we just need to assign characters." Lois tapped her finger against her chin as she studied her cast. "We'll need three shepherds. Irwin, you look like you could herd sheep. Care to step into the role?"

The sheriff looked relieved to not have to play a child. "Of course."

"What about you, Garth?"

"I do work with animals."

"Can you get us some live sheep?"

Garth thought for a moment. "I'm not sure. I can try."

Lois pointed to Martin. "And you and Oliver, can you be the wise men?" They glanced at each other.

"I think so," Martin shrugged. "I do have a way with gold."

"I'll take the myrrh."

"Perfect. We can recruit another shepherd and another wise man as stand-ins. They won't need to speak."

"What about the innkeeper?" Martin asked. Everyone started offering suggestions, but Wolfe couldn't take any more. He wasn't going to do this play, and the only thing on his mind was Ainsley. Wolfe gathered his things from the dressing room.

"Wolfe?" Lois stood in the doorway, blocking his exit. "I know this sounds a little crazy, but—"

Wolfe waved his hand. "Lois, you don't understand. You can't possibly understand."

She walked over and knelt next to him. Looking up, she put a gentle hand on his arm. "Play Joseph."

"What?"

"Please. Nobody else can pull off that role, Wolfe. You're perfect for it. You can do it."

Wolfe shook his head. "Lois, I've been in this town a long time, but this is the craziest thing I've ever heard of."

Lois grinned. "I know! It's a rush, isn't it? But Wolfe, don't you see it? Sure, Alfred messed up big time. But maybe, just maybe, this isn't a mistake."

"I think you could use a nap and a good dose of reality."

"Possibly. Right now I sort of feel like I'm hovering, but that's beside the point."

"Then what's the point, Lois? Tell me the point."

"The point is that everyone is eager to hear about the greatest event in history, the day that God came down to earth to rescue His people. That's what they're coming to see. And that's what we have to do." She squeezed his hand. "Wolfe, please. Play Joseph. Please."

Wolfe was about to shake his head and bolt for the door, but suddenly an idea came over him.

"What do you say, Wolfe? Will you do it?"

"On one condition."

"What?"

"You get Ainsley to play Mary."

CHAPTER 20

Are these the shadows of the things that Will be, or
are they shadows of the things that May be, only?

"CAN SOMEBODY MOVE that pig to stage right?" Lois yelled over the noise.

"He doesn't want to be near the donkey!" someone yelled back.

"Then get the donkey off the stage. It'll carry Mary down this aisle. Has anyone located Mary?"

"Not yet," Oliver said. "Melb is trying to find her."

Suddenly Alfred was beside her. He regarded the scene before him, then sat down next to Lois. "I can't believe you're actually doing this," Alfred said.

"Me either," Lois said. "But I can't describe how it feels. It's a huge adrenaline rush!"

Alfred studied the actors. "They do look rather…biblical."

"I know! Isn't it amazing? Turned wrong side out, most of the costumes look exactly like dusty old garments! Katelyn has tons of stuff she's been hot-gluing on to help. Never thought the BeDazzler would come in so handy. For the last hour, people have been bringing in everything from staffs for the shepherds to crowns for the wise men." Suddenly, Lois turned to him. "You! Yes, you!"

"Me, what?"

"I still don't have an innkeeper."

"Oh...no. No. Lois, seriously. I couldn't."

"Yes you can. Alfred, you got us into this mess, the least you can do is turn Mary away and order her to the barn."

"But...but..."

"It'll be fine. I'll play the innkeeper's wife, and between the two of us, we'll work it out."

Alfred swallowed hard as he looked at the stage. "I suppose it is the least I can do."

"Great! Go backstage and look through the Dracula costumes. That's about all that's left, unless nobody claimed Quasimodo."

Alfred stood. "I feel like I'm having an out-of-body experience."

Lois smiled. "Me too."

Two hours until show time, and they still couldn't find Ainsley. Sick to his stomach with worry, Wolfe could barely concentrate on what he was supposed to be doing, which was pretty unclear to begin with.

Taking the Bible, Lois had broken the story down into several simple scenes. Some of the actors were playing more than one role, which confused matters even further. And Wolfe couldn't help thinking this was some cruel joke. Dickens was spared, but now he would be made a fool for God.

Truthfully, he didn't care. He just wanted to see Ainsley. He'd hoped that if Lois had called upon her to play Mary, that would get her to the theater. But so far, it hadn't worked.

Clasping his hands together, Wolfe bowed his head. He'd been so angry at all the nonsense, he'd forgotten to pray at all about any of it. He didn't know what to say, except to ask for God's help.

"You're going to do fine, dude." Wolfe looked up. Dustin stood there, dressed in white. "Isn't this awesome? It's an old ghost costume I had from the store. Mrs. Downey added some glitter and *bam*! I'm Gabriel!"

"You're Gabriel?"

Dustin shrugged. "They thought my long, wavy hair had nice appeal."

"Great."

"You're creative, man. You're in your element, except you're not creating on paper. You're creating onstage, dude! This is going to be fantastic. Anything can happen out there!"

"I know," Wolfe sighed. "That's the problem."

Dustin sat down. "Think of it as a book. What would the characters do? Say? That's all this is, man! It's like the ultimate plot twist!"

"Yes, well, it would be helpful if they could find my wife. The Christmas story can be told a lot of different ways, but not without Mary."

"Melb Stepaphanolopolis volunteered for the role. You know, just in case Ainsley doesn't show up."

Wolfe rolled his eyes. "Terrific."

Oliver suddenly burst through the curtain. "Wolfe! We found her!"

Clutching Abigail, Ainsley made her way down the aisle of the theater, escorted by two of her father's deputies. They led her to Lois, whose tousled hair had two pencils sticking out of it. She was shouting directions and pointing this way and that with a third pencil. "Lois," one of the deputies said, and she turned.

"Ainsley! Thank goodness!"

"I don't understand," Ainsley said, eyeing the… Was that a *pig*? "What's happening?"

"Short on time. Will explain later. Need you to be Mary, the mother of God. Can you or can't you?"

"But…what…I don't…"

"Okay, that's not how you play her. Mary needs to be serene and pulled together, do you understand? She appears frightened once, when the angel comes to see her. After that, she's solid as a rock."

"I thought this was a—"

"Yes, well, Dickens is overrated. We're going with God. You know the story by heart. Here's a basic rundown of the play," she said, shoving a piece of paper into Ainsley's hand. "We've got a costume waiting for you backstage. Ignore the bloodstain. It's fake, but we'll need to make reference to it sometime during the play. Maybe you cut your finger as you fell backward in awe."

Lois gestured like she was thinking out loud, then stopped and turned toward the stage. "I know what's missing! I've got it. How did I not think about this before?" She grabbed one of the deputies. "You. Go get the reverend. Now! And tell him to dress like he would for a funeral!"

He hurried off, and Lois grabbed Ainsley by the shoulder, leading her up onstage. "Mary's here, people. And the lines are starting to form outside. We've got one shot at this! But do not fear! God is bringing us a helper!"

She led Ainsley backstage and took Abigail out of her arms,

handing her to a woman nearby who was trying to make a star from cardboard. "Ainsley, listen to me. I know this is a little unsettling. Believe me. We're all feeling the pressure. But you can do this. Now, let me help set the character for you. Think pure. A little naive. Definitely virgin. But she's got gumption, okay? She's confident, but not cocky. Beautiful, but not aware of it. Okay? Heck, Ainsley, just play yourself, all right?"

"But who is Joseph?"

"Who else? Wolfe! Perfect, huh?"

"But, no. I can't. We're not…we're…"

"Lois! The sheep have arrived!"

"Excuse me for a moment. Get your costume on pronto! I'll be back in a second." Lois rushed off, and Ainsley looked around. She spotted Wolfe standing nearby. Tears formed in her eyes, but she couldn't say anything. She was overwhelmed enough as it was. He started to come over, but Ainsley shook her head and turned, swiping a tear off her face. *This* was the last thing she needed, to be pulled into an insane production with Wolfe playing her husband. It was just a reminder that he might've been playing this role all along. Sniffling, she tried to compose herself.

For now, she was nobody's wife—just a woman, alone, afraid, and with a child.

CHAPTER 21

> "At this time of the rolling year," the spectre said, "I suffer most. Why did I walk through crowds of fellow-beings with my eyes turned down, and never raise them to that blessed Star which led the Wise Men to a poor abode! Were there no poor homes to which its light would have conducted me!"

LOIS PEEKED THROUGH the curtain, then turned back to the actors clustered around her. "The house is packed! People are standing in the back!" She held up her hands. "Everyone stay calm. This situation is totally under control. Right, Reverend?"

Everyone looked at the reverend, who stood in stunned silence.

"Reverend?"

He just shook his head. "I don't think I can do this. I haven't prepared. I don't—know what to say, and I might mess up. This could be—"

"Reverend, you know this story inside and out! You preach about it every single Christmas, don't you?"

"Yes, but—"

"Just get up there, and pretend that's a crowd full of people in your pews."

Suddenly, the reverend's entire demeanor changed. He started to smile. "This is it!" he said, with a sudden burst of enthusiasm. "This is the miracle!"

"What miracle?" someone asked.

Lois answered. "Just roll with it, people. If the rev says it's a miracle, then it's a miracle. It's certainly going to take one to pull this thing off. Now, bow your heads, everyone. Beg God for His help, and let's take our places!"

They dimmed the house lights, and the crowd grew quiet. Lois cued Ainsley and the reverend toward the stage. She turned to the reverend. "God be with you." And then she shoved him onto the stage.

"Lights up," Lois instructed.

The reverend was caught off guard by the glaring light in his face. He couldn't even see the people out there as he squinted like a flashbulb had just gone off. But he could hear them, and they were starting to whisper as he stood there. He glanced back at Ainsley, who looked equally terrified. Her eyes bounced from him toward the audience, as she sat and clutched her robe, which was far too long and pooled at her feet.

The reverend turned back to the crowd and said, "She was terrified."

The crowd murmured, but he tried a confident expression. "As anyone would be if they were visited by an angel."

"Cue angel!" he heard Lois whisper, and suddenly, Dustin stumbled onto the stage, glancing backward and scowling, while adjusting his shiny gold belt. Apparently trying to seem more angelic, he grinned widely as he approached Mary.

"The angel said to Mary, 'Greetings, favored woman! The Lord is with you!' "

Dustin nodded and looked at Mary, pitching a thumbs-up.

The reverend continued. "Mary was frightened and"—he looked back—"trembling. 'Don't be afraid! The Lord has decided to bless you!' "

Dustin's confidence surged. "You're going to get pregnant. This will totally freak you out because, of course, you're a virgin. But this is the way God wants it. And He's going to do all these cool things like—"

"You will name Him Jesus," the reverend inserted, "and He will be very great and will be called the Son of the Most High. And the Lord will give Him the throne of his ancestor David. He will reign over Israel forever; His kingdom will never end!"

The reverend smiled at Ainsley. She knew this by heart; he could see it in her eyes. Rising, Ainsley looked at Dustin. "But how can I have a baby? I am a virgin."

"That's the cool thing—," Dustin started.

"The Holy Spirit will come upon you, and the power of the Most High will overshadow you. This baby born to you will be holy, and He will be called the Son of God. Also, your relative Elizabeth has become pregnant in her old age! People used to say she was barren, but she's already in her sixth month! For nothing is impossible with God."

Thankfully, Dustin looked at a loss for words.

"I am the Lord's servant," Ainsley said, "and I am willing to accept whatever He wants. May everything you have said come true."

"And the angel left," the reverend said. Dustin sighed and skulked offstage.

"Cue Elizabeth!" Lois whispered.

Melb entered from stage right. Lois had fastened a basketball underneath her robe to make her look pregnant. As she walked toward Mary, she groaned. "Oh, my! I just can't describe to you what it's like to be pregnant at my age! It's killing my feet. And my back? I can't even sleep on my side anymore. You want to talk about stretch marks? Honey, when you're my age—"

"Suddenly, Elizabeth's baby leaped within her, and Elizabeth was filled with the Holy Spirit."

Melb bumped the ball up a little with her thumbs. She gazed at the ceiling and lifted her arms up like she might take flight.

"Um…and Elizabeth said to Mary, 'You have been blessed by God above all other women, and your child is blessed.' "

Suddenly Ainsley burst into tears. "I know. I know! I want to believe it!"

The reverend cleared his throat. He was pretty sure Mary was supposed to be joyful, but he rolled with it. "And Elizabeth and Mary quickly went offstage to rejoice!"

Melb dropped her arms, looked at Ainsley, and hurried her offstage left, but not before the basketball fell out of her stomach and bounced to stage right. The lights went down, and Lois cued Joseph onstage. The reverend watched Wolfe pretend to work on a wooden table that had at one time belonged to the Cratchit family.

"Cue lights! Cue Mary!"

Ainsley slowly walked onstage, still wiping her tears. She looked at the reverend as she blotted her nose with a Kleenex.

The reverend tried to fill in the silence. "Mary didn't know how to tell Joseph. How could he understand such a thing?"

Wolfe stood and faced Ainsley. "Hello, Mary."

"Hello, Joseph."

"How are you?"

"Oh, um, fine. How are you?"

"Just working on my table here." He smiled and gestured toward it. "What do you think?"

"I'm pregnant, and the baby isn't yours. It's God's. I don't expect you to believe me or stay with me. It's hard enough to have a baby in wedlock, as you might imagine. So I don't expect you to deal with this mess. And that's what this is going to be, Joseph. A real mess. Okay?" She turned and stomped off the stage. Wolfe glanced at the reverend for help.

"Uh…then an angel of the Lord appeared to Joseph in a dream…"

"Cue angel!"

Wolfe laid down by his table and curled up as Dustin floated back onstage. "Joseph, wake up! Hey, wake up!"

"In a dream…" the reverend urged.

"Oh. Oops."

"The angel said, 'Do not be afraid to take Mary as your wife. The baby she carries is from God. You must name the child Jesus because He will save the people from their sins.' "

Wolfe pretended to wake up from this dream. But all the pondering in the world couldn't save this scene, and just as the angel was about to say something, Lois killed the lights.

The reverend wasn't sure what to do next, so he just stood in the dark. Soon enough, though, he heard the sounds of a donkey.

"Cue donkey, Mary, Joseph!"

Out they came, Ainsley riding on the donkey and looking absolutely terrified as she clutched its ears. Wolfe held a string that was supposed to be a rope. The donkey wore the most fascinating expression of the three of them.

"Now in those days, Caesar Augustus, the Roman ruler, decreed that a census should be taken throughout the Roman Empire. All returned to their own towns to register for this census. Because Joseph was a descendant of King David, he had to go to Bethlehem, in Judea. He traveled there from Nazareth, taking Mary, his pregnant fiancée, with him."

They crossed the stage and exited without a word and the lights went down. The reverend could hear the crowd grumbling. "This is stupid!" one person said. Another growled, "What a waste of money!"

"Cue animals!"

Suddenly chickens, pigs, a miniature horse, and a few cats entered the stage, all making a racket. But to the reverend's surprise, the audience began chuckling with delight. After two hay bales were pushed onstage, the lights came up. The reverend heard Lois whisper, "Not yet!" and the lights came back down.

A pig waddled up beside him. The reverend really hoped, at this point, he might be upstaged by an animal.

Alfred was already sweating like a pig, even before the hundreds of eyes he was responsible for bringing directed their attention to him.

Lois had opted out of being the innkeeper's wife, claiming she didn't have enough good lines, which left Alfred alone in the inn.

"Um…I'm sorry…" Alfred said, gesturing toward the hay. "This is all I have. Just a stable. You should've gotten here earlier, but unfortunately, there's no room in the inn." Alfred sighed with relief. He'd managed to pull off his lines.

"Can you get us some blankets?" Joseph suddenly asked.

"Oh…uh…" Alfred tried to remember the Bible story the best he could, but nothing came to him. He was fairly certain, though, that the innkeeper was uncooperative. "Sorry. We're out of blankets."

"What about something to eat? My wife…fiancée—it's a long story—anyway, we have traveled a great distance, and she is about to give birth. Please, if we could just have a tiny morsel of food."

"Fresh out of food, I'm afraid." The pig oinked. "Except bacon."

"We don't eat bacon."

"Why?"

"Never mind," said Joseph. "Mary is mine to look after. And I will. I will take care of her for the rest of her life and not let anything harm her. God gave her to me, and I love her very much." Wolfe looked at Ainsley, and his eyes filled with tears.

The audience gasped with emotion, and Alfred glanced at them, then tried to get back into his character. But what more could he say? He realized he was now the antagonist of the play. He decided that instant that he would get the forthcoming child a blanket. Yes, he had something to give, though it was small.

But right as he was about to offer it, the reverend butted in. "And so the innkeeper left." A few people actually clapped, and Alfred could do nothing but turn and walk offstage.

"Cue wise men! They're coming from the back of the theater!"

"Lois, wait!" Alfred said. "Please. Let me go back on. I want to give the child a blanket."

Lois was helping hoist the star. "What are you talking about? Your part is over. You did fine. Now go help with costume changes or something." Alfred watched her hurry toward Ainsley, who bounced Ollie around like a carnival ride, trying to keep him from crying.

"Listen to me, Ainsley," Lois said. "This transition is tricky. We're going to have to give the audience the illusion you're really giving birth."

"Can't I just go out there carrying the baby? They'll get the idea."

"Ainsley, for the sake of women everywhere, we owe them this. Babies just don't pop out. And Mary was in a stable, for crying out loud. So imagine no epidural and a bed full of hay."

"I...I can't. I can't—"

The lights suddenly came up and Alfred watched Lois's eyes grow wide with panic.

"Ahhhhh!" Lois screamed. "Ahhh! Ohhh! Ahhh!"

Alfred rushed to her. "Lois, are you okay?"

"Don't tell me to push, you moron! You push! You try this for one second! Ohhh! The pain! The pain!" She turned to Ainsley and whispered. "Now, go out there and sit next to the hay. Put the baby in that trough and whatever you do, don't let him cry."

"Why?" Ainsley asked.

"It's baby Jesus! He didn't cry! Keep looking serene. Tilt your head a little. Glow from within. And wait for the wise men. Lights up! *Go*!"

Lois watched Ainsley from the side of the stage, but Alfred couldn't shake the urge that he needed to do something more. He touched her elbow. "Lois, please. I need to give the baby something."

Lois turned to him. "Why, Alfred?"

Alfred paused, trying to understand it himself. "Because, if God can use a mess like this," he said, gesturing toward the stage, "then maybe He can use a mess like me."

Lois's eyes narrowed, and Alfred realized he'd just called this production a mess. It was fairly obvious to everyone, but nothing ever seemed obvious with Lois.

"Alfred, the wise men are already en route. There's nothing I can do."

Onstage, he could hear the reverend. "About that time, some wise men from eastern lands arrived in Jerusalem. Scripturally, they didn't actually arrive at His birth. It was several years later, but for the sake of time, the traditional nativity has them coming when He was a baby..."

"Oh, brother," Lois sighed.

Finally, the reverend got back on track. " 'Where is the newborn king of the Jews? We have seen His star as it arose, and we have come to worship Him...' "

Suddenly, a voice crackled through the radio. "Lois, Frankincense has passed out!"

"What?"

"The deli guy," said Oliver. "I think he passed out from fear!"

"Where are you?"

"Outside. We're just about to come in." The radio crackled. "Lois, what do we do?"

Lois turned to Alfred. "I guess this is your chance. Your sign. Go out the back door and run around the building. Grab the frankincense and follow the pack!"

Without hesitation, Alfred hurried outdoors. The freezing wind hit him hard, but he raced around the building. Oliver and Martin were hovering over the deli guy. "He's waking up."

Alfred yanked the heavy gold necklaces off his neck and grabbed the box he had been carrying. "Come on. We have no time! We must go!" The men hurried through the doors. The audience turned as they entered.

Each man slowed his stride and steadied his hands as the group methodically walked toward the baby.

"The star appeared to them, guiding them to Bethlehem."

The star popped up over the curtains, fell with a crash, and then popped back up again.

"It went ahead of them and stopped over the place where the child was. When they saw the star, they were filled with joy!" Alfred smiled. He couldn't help it, but he didn't really know why. "They found the child and His mother Mary and worshiped Him."

The three men walked onto the stage. Oliver and Martin immediately went before the baby and knelt. Alfred followed, kneeling a few feet away. Something strange was happening in his heart. He couldn't understand it. Maybe it was stage fright, except he wasn't feeling afraid. In fact, he was feeling hopeful. Joyful. Energized.

What once seemed dormant inside him awakened, like a spring flower popping through the winter's cold earth. He was reading the sheet music…and understanding it.

He clutched the box he held and listened to the reverend narrate.

"Then the wise men opened their treasure chests. One gave Him gold, because He was king." Martin moved forward, setting the gold—once Scrooge's—down in front of the baby.

"One gave Him myrrh, because He was man." Oliver stepped forward and put his box down.

Alfred rose, walked over, and knelt before the baby. He looked at Ainsley and Wolfe, and tears filled his eyes. Was this what Wolfe felt all those years before, what he'd left everything for? This baby that would save the world from their sins?

Tears dripped down Alfred's face as he gently placed the small wooden box in front of the manger. It seemed inadequate. Behind him, he could hear people weeping. He heard the reverend say, "And one gave Him frankincense...because He was God."

Alfred clasped his hands together, closed his eyes and whispered, "I'm sorry. Forgive me! I've been a fool. I've chased after the unimportant things in life, while people suffered needlessly around me. I am a horrible man," Alfred wept. "I am a horrible man."

The audience held its breath, and the only sound onstage was Alfred, finally revealing the weak and insecure man that he was. He felt a hand on his shoulder. Alfred looked up, and Wolfe's gentle eyes locked with his. "God loves you. He sent His Son to save you. To save me. To save all of us from our sins."

Alfred wiped his eyes. "I have nothing to give but what's in this box." He looked down and opened it. A Yankee candle and some incense.

"All God wants you to give Him is you. You are far more valuable than all these treasures," Ainsley said.

Alfred slowly closed the box. Though the tears would not stop, he felt a freedom in his heart that he'd never known. The kind that let him cry in front of a group of strangers and not care an ounce. He stood up and grabbed Wolfe, pulling him into a hug. "Thank you."

"Cue shepherds!"

Alfred looked at the tiny child one more time, then at the mother he knew would someday lose Him to a violent death caused by Alfred's own sin, and walked offstage to roaring applause.

CHAPTER 22

"MOVE IT, PEOPLE! Get out there. Shepherds on the left. Wise men on the right. Get that pig out of the way. Somebody get the pig out of the way! Mary, dear, you've got hay in your hair. Mary cannot have hay in her hair!" Lois pointed all over the place. "People, this is the last scene! We cannot blow it! Get into place! Come on! Hurry!"

Lois adjusted Gabriel's halo as they herded the animals back onstage and erected the star again. "Hurry! On! Go!" she barked at Dustin. She turned to Wolfe and Ainsley. "What are you doing? Get out there! We have to have the nativity scene complete! Animals! Angels! Wise men! Shepherds!" She shoved them toward the entrance to the stage, but suddenly they all smelled something.

"Is that the donkey?" Wolfe asked.

Lois shook her head and pointed down at Ollie. "It's him. Oh, heavens, no! We cannot have the baby Jesus with a diaper problem!"

Wolfe reached for Abigail, who was being rocked by a woman backstage. They exchanged babies, and Wolfe suddenly wanted nothing more than to rock his daughter in his arms.

"Get *out* there!" Lois barked. "We can't have a nativity scene without Mary, Joseph, and Jesus."

Wolfe stopped and turned to her. "Lois, I know I've given you no reason to trust me. I've pestered you to death about the way you want your play to go. But you've turned this production into something special, and I want to... I mean, I'm asking your permission to do something a little different. After the lights come on, I'd like to walk out with Ainsley and the baby."

Lois glanced at the stage, then smiled. "You know me. I like 'a little different.' *Cue lights*!"

The lights came on, and Ainsley looked up at Wolfe. He took her by the elbow and said, "Trust me."

He let a few seconds go by, then he guided Ainsley and the baby to the center of the stage. He nodded to the reverend, who took his cue to step back. Then he turned to Ainsley and cupped her face in his. "Mary, I'm sorry."

"Sorry? For what?"

"For ever making you feel that I didn't want you. Or our baby. I was confused for a while. And weary. But I love you. And I love our baby. I know that you are both gifts from God. I promise to treasure you through it all, through the good times and the bad, through the desert and the mountains, and never to take you for granted, no matter what."

Ainsley reached up and pulled him into a kiss. To a standing ovation, Wolfe led his wife to the stable, where they were surrounded by their friends and family. Ainsley grinned as she set Abigail into the manger. Camera flashes lit the air as cheering ensued. Wolfe raised his hand, quieting the crowd, and in a loud voice exclaimed, *"It was always said of him that he knew how to keep Christmas well, if any man alive possessed the knowledge. May that be truly said of us—and all of us! God bless us, every one!"*

The crowd cheered, and the cast looked for Lois to come take a bow, but she was curled up in a ball near stage right, fast asleep.

> It is a fair, even-handed, noble adjustment of things, that while there is infection in disease and sorrow, there is nothing in the world so irresistibly contagious as laughter and good-humour.

THE END

ACKNOWLEDGMENTS

FIRST I WANT to acknowledge the fans of the Boo Series. Without all of you, *Boo* would've been a single book. But your love for the characters and town of Skary inspired me to dig deeper for more stories. So many more were found! Thanks for your loyalty.

Also, my thanks to Shannon Hill, Laura Wright, and the mighty and creative team at WaterBrook. I appreciate all of you. You are gifted at what you do, and I appreciate all your work on behalf of this series. I'd also like to mention Mark Ford and the design team for coming up with these unforgettable covers.

Special thanks to my sister, Wendy, who birthed this idea when she suggested the title at Christmas dinner. And thanks as always to my agent, a warm, friendly, wise voice, always available on the other end of the phone.

Last, and with much love, thanks to Sean, John Caleb, and Cate, who fill my home with irresistibly contagious laughter and good humor. Praise be to God who fills our hearts with joy.

About the Author

Rene Gutteridge is the author of thirteen novels. She worked as a church playwright and drama director, writing over five hundred short sketches, before publishing her first novel and deciding to stay home with her first child.

Rene is married to Sean, a musician, and enjoys raising their two children while writing full time. She also enjoys helping new writers and teaching at writers' conferences. She and her family make their home in Oklahoma.

Please visit her Web site at www.renegutteridge.com.